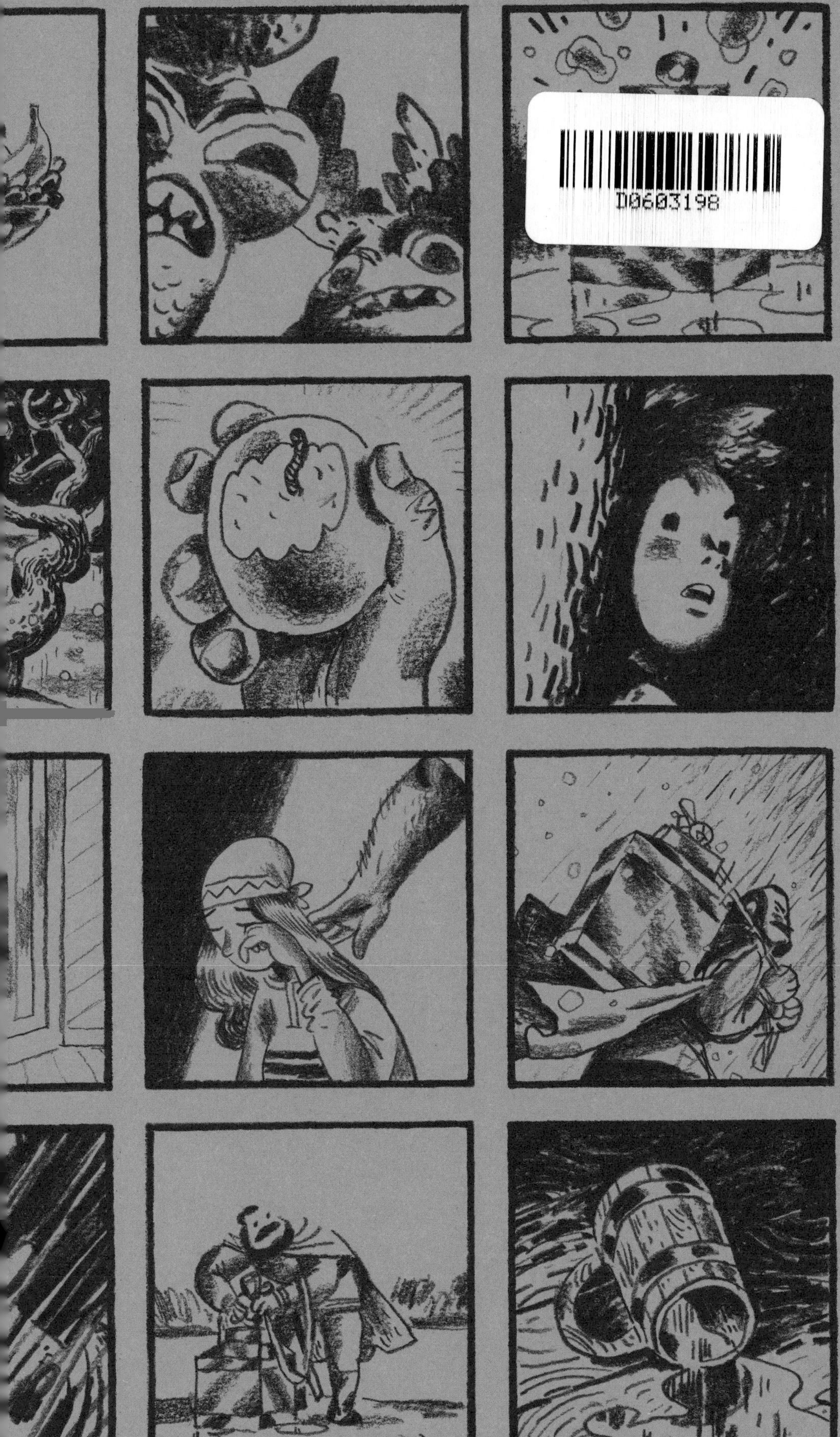

TO MY PARENTS, FRIENDS,
HAYAO & GORO MIYAZAKI.

GAMAYUN
TALES

BASED ON RUSSIAN
FOLK TALES

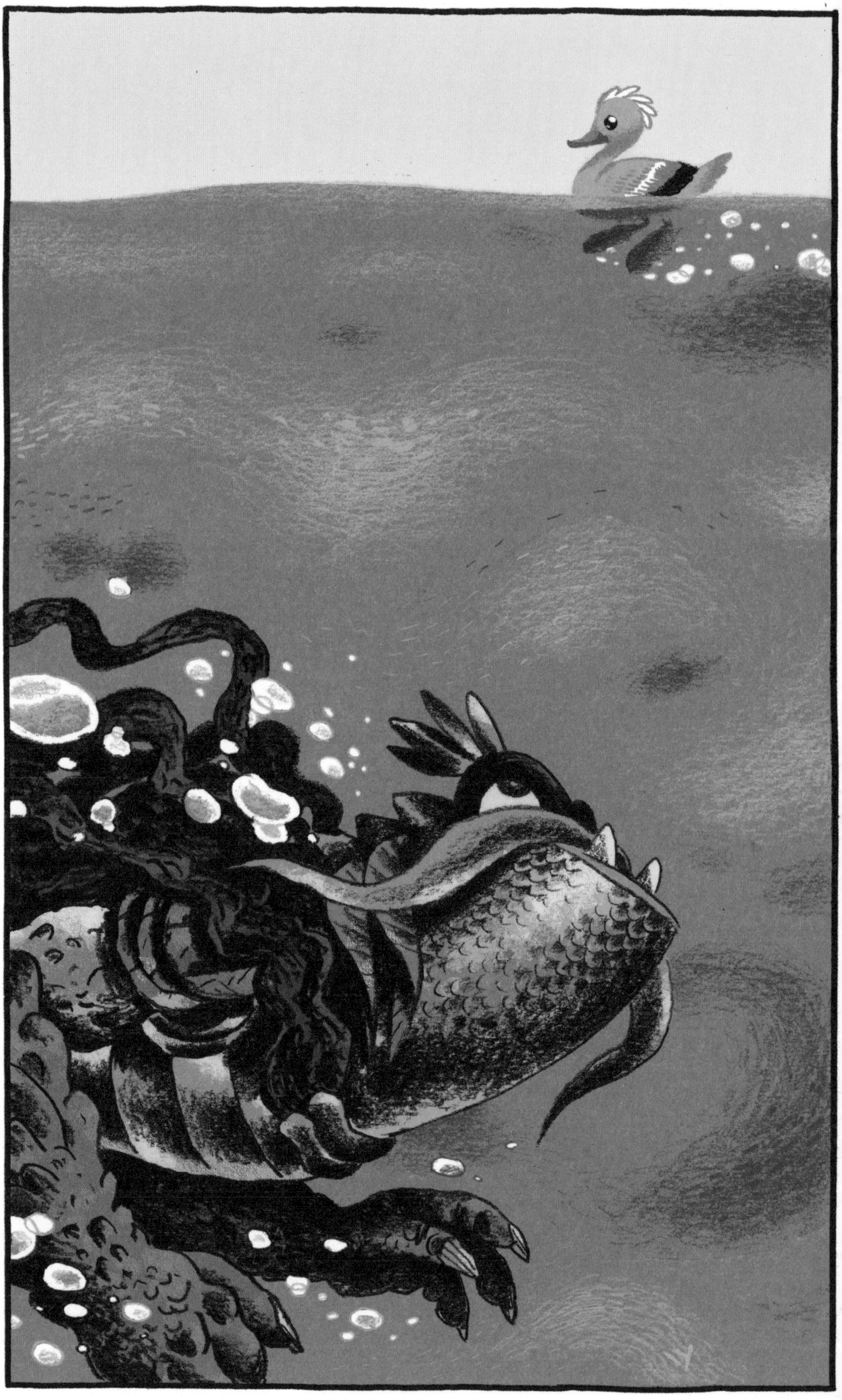

THE WATER SPIRIT

WRITTEN & DRAWN BY
ALEXANDER UTKIN

TRANSLATED BY
LADA MOROZOVA

NOBROW
LONDON | NEW YORK

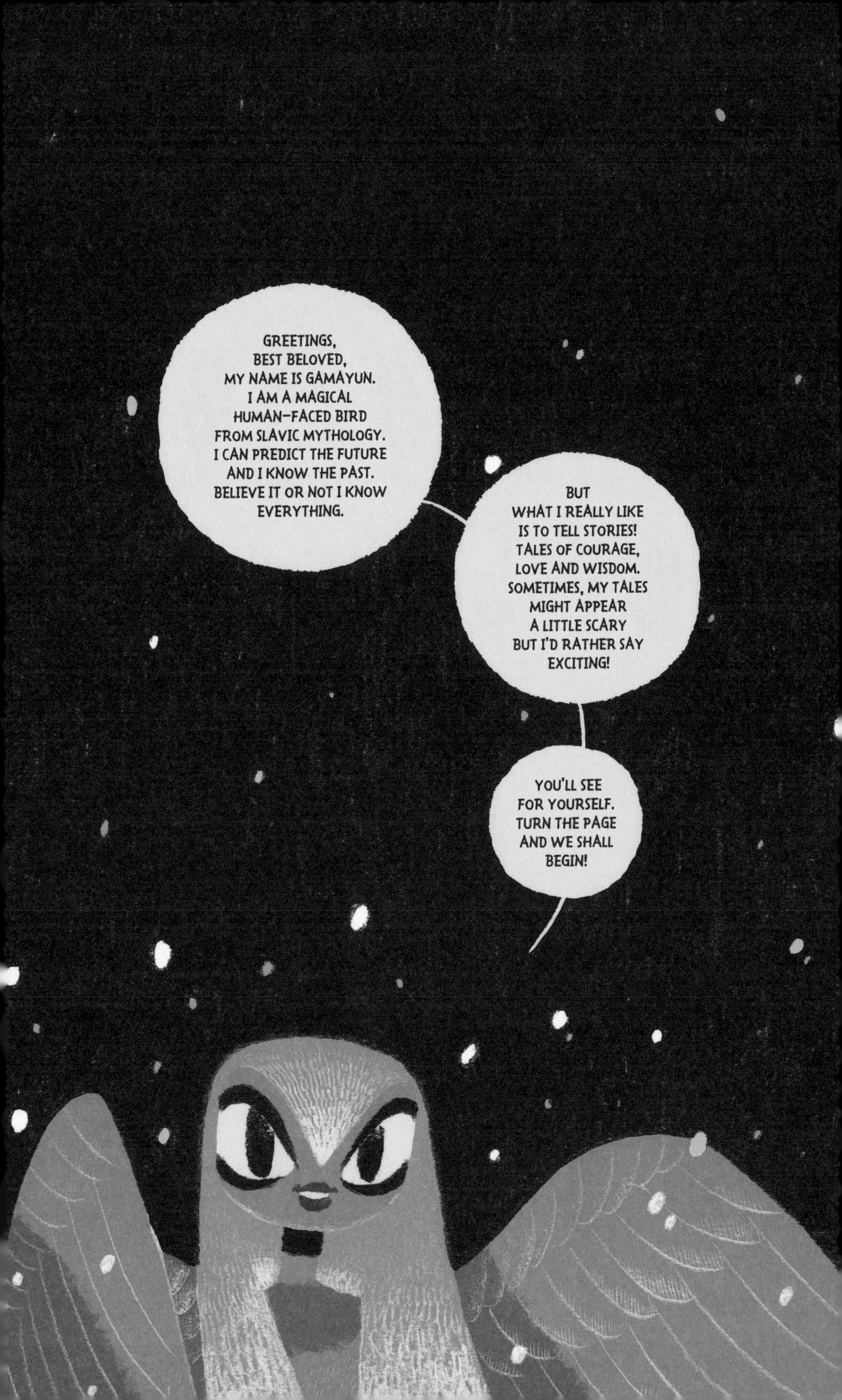
GREETINGS, BEST BELOVED, MY NAME IS GAMAYUN. I AM A MAGICAL HUMAN-FACED BIRD FROM SLAVIC MYTHOLOGY. I CAN PREDICT THE FUTURE AND I KNOW THE PAST. BELIEVE IT OR NOT I KNOW EVERYTHING.
BUT WHAT I REALLY LIKE IS TO TELL STORIES! TALES OF COURAGE, LOVE AND WISDOM. SOMETIMES, MY TALES MIGHT APPEAR A LITTLE SCARY BUT I'D RATHER SAY EXCITING!
YOU'LL SEE FOR YOURSELF. TURN THE PAGE AND WE SHALL BEGIN!

THE GOLDEN CHEST

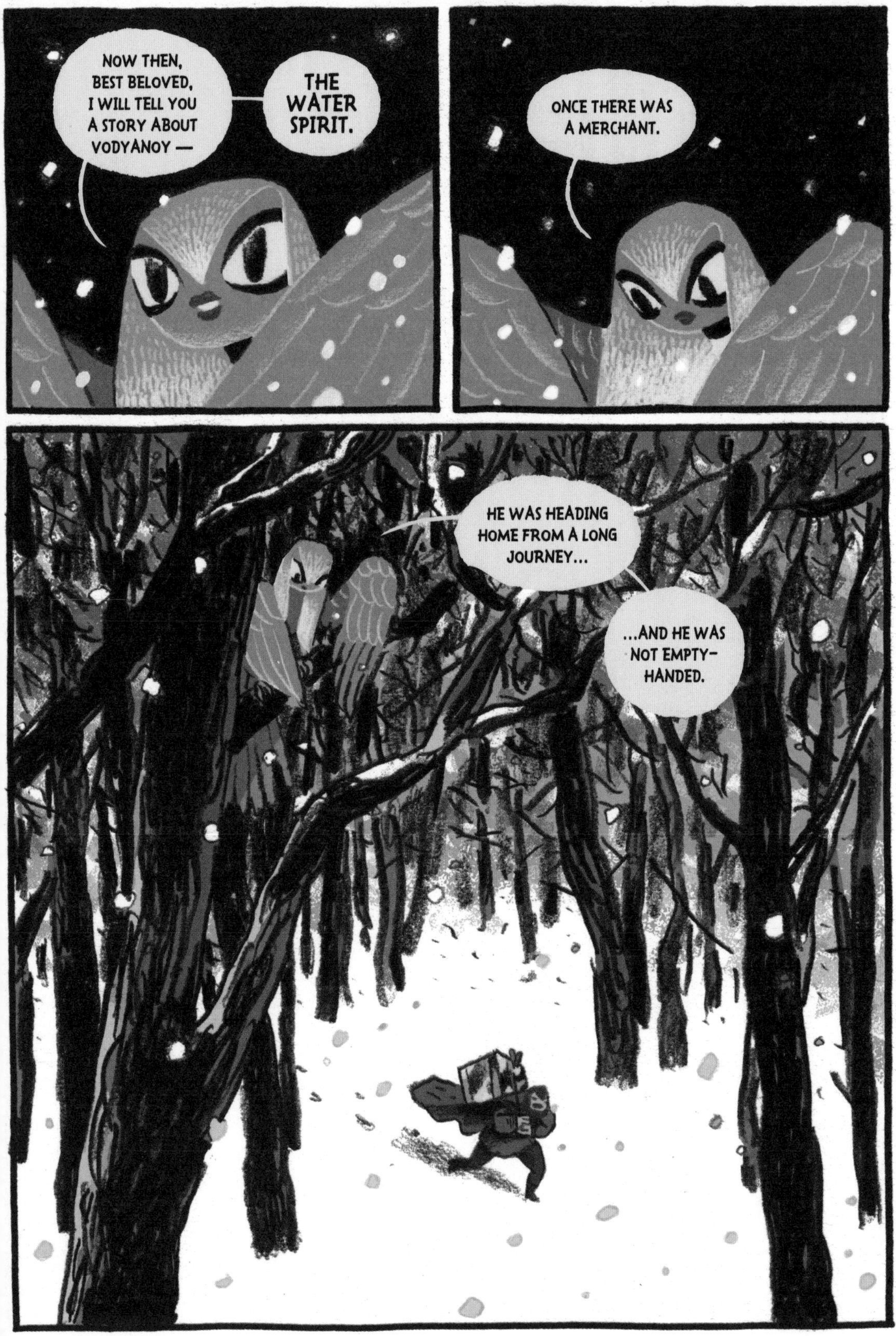
NOW THEN, BEST BELOVED, I WILL TELL YOU A STORY ABOUT VODYANOY —
THE WATER SPIRIT.
ONCE THERE WAS A MERCHANT.
HE WAS HEADING HOME FROM A LONG JOURNEY...
...AND HE WAS NOT EMPTY-HANDED.

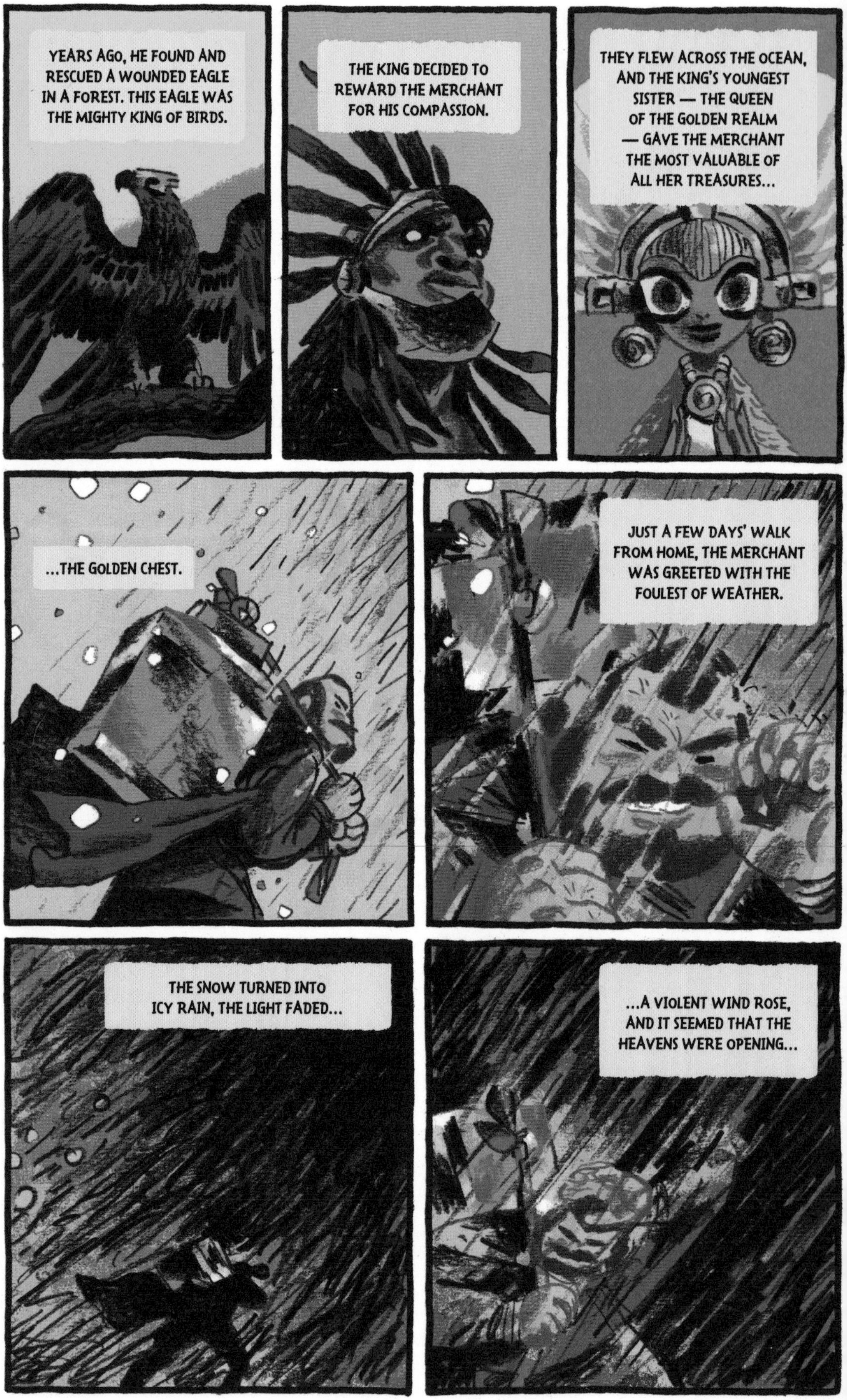
YEARS AGO, HE FOUND AND RESCUED A WOUNDED EAGLE IN A FOREST. THIS EAGLE WAS THE MIGHTY KING OF BIRDS.
THE KING DECIDED TO REWARD THE MERCHANT FOR HIS COMPASSION.
THEY FLEW ACROSS THE OCEAN, AND THE KING'S YOUNGEST SISTER — THE QUEEN OF THE GOLDEN REALM — GAVE THE MERCHANT THE MOST VALUABLE OF ALL HER TREASURES...
...THE GOLDEN CHEST.
JUST A FEW DAYS' WALK FROM HOME, THE MERCHANT WAS GREETED WITH THE FOULEST OF WEATHER.
THE SNOW TURNED INTO ICY RAIN, THE LIGHT FADED...
...A VIOLENT WIND ROSE, AND IT SEEMED THAT THE HEAVENS WERE OPENING...

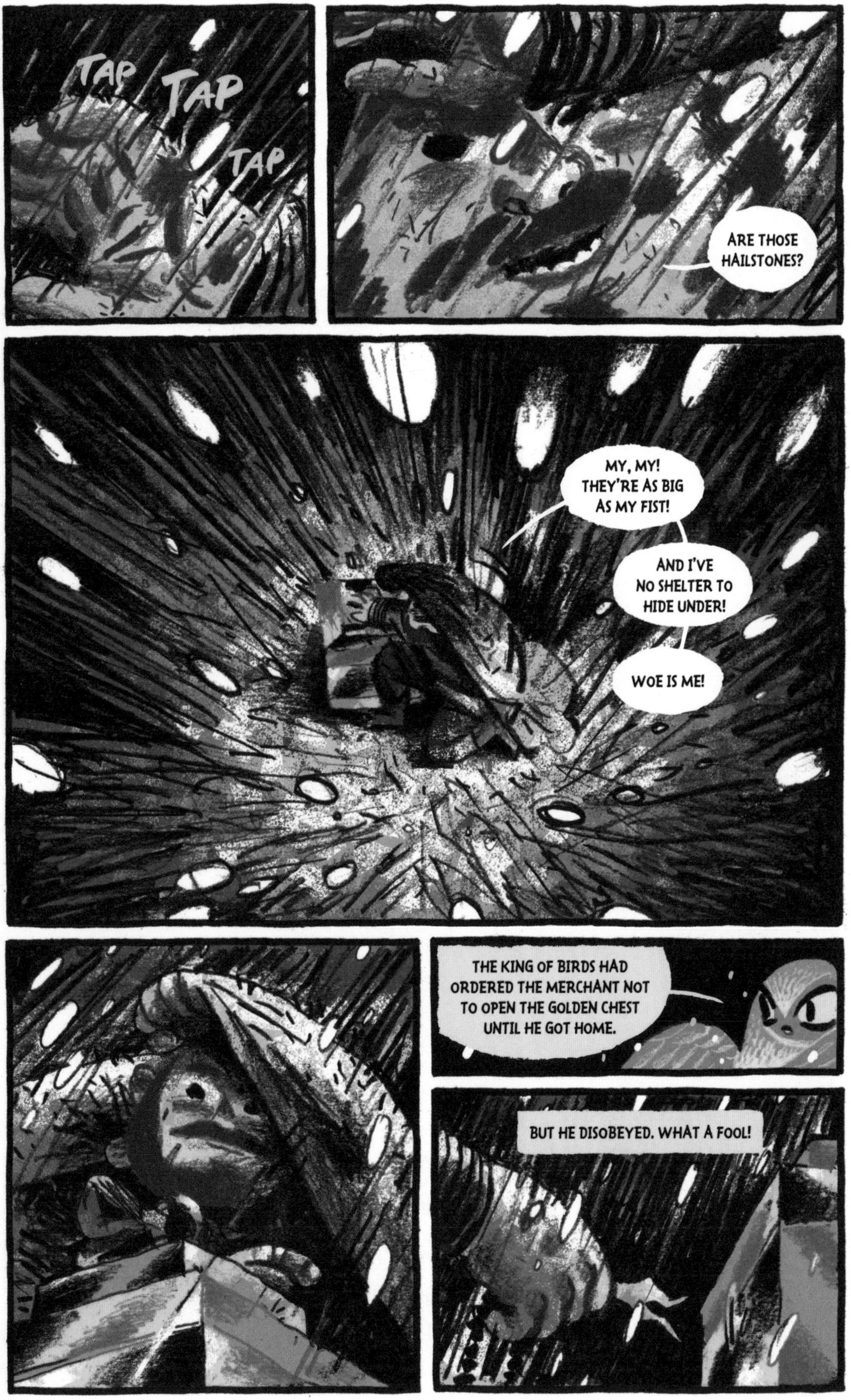
TAP TAP TAP
ARE THOSE HAILSTONES?
MY, MY! THEY'RE AS BIG AS MY FIST!
AND I'VE NO SHELTER TO HIDE UNDER!
WOE IS ME!
THE KING OF BIRDS HAD ORDERED THE MERCHANT NOT TO OPEN THE GOLDEN CHEST UNTIL HE GOT HOME.
BUT HE DISOBEYED. WHAT A FOOL!

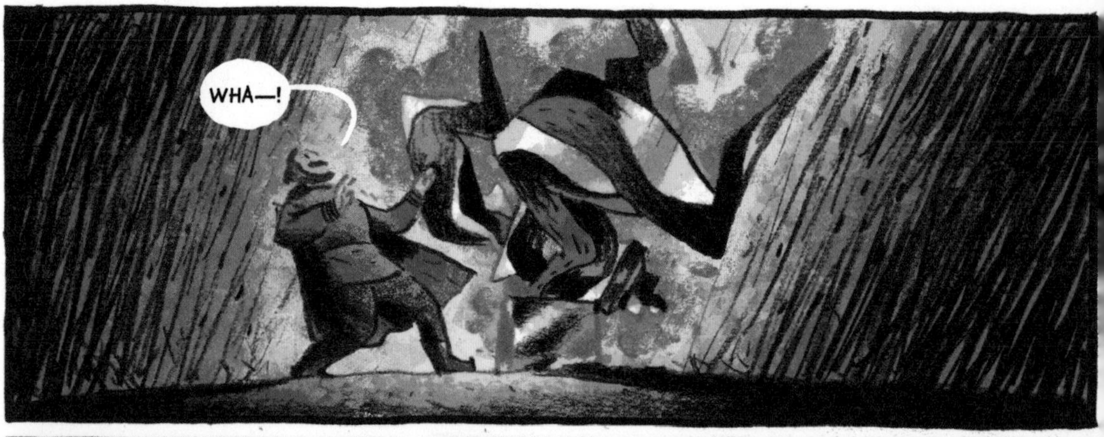
WHA—!

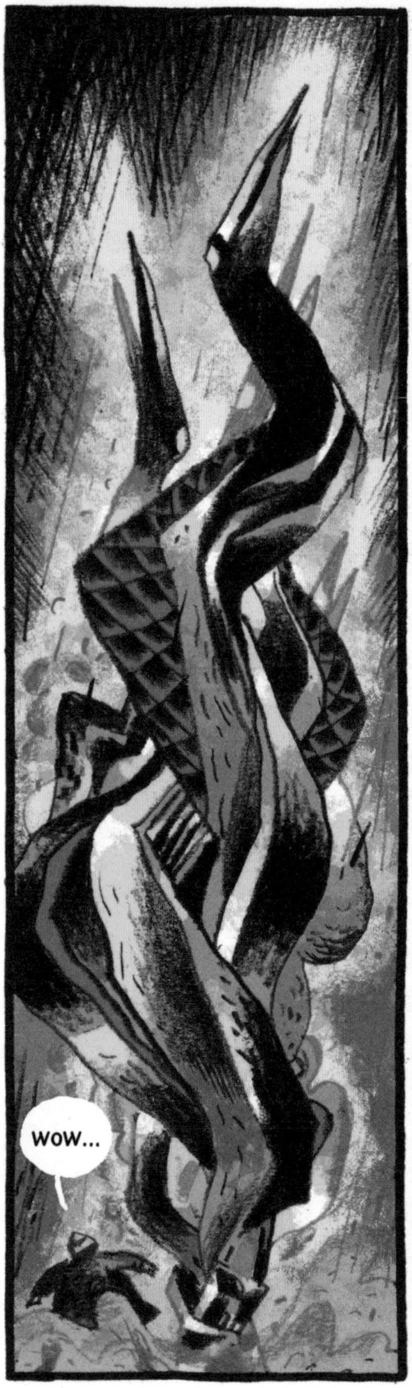
WOW...

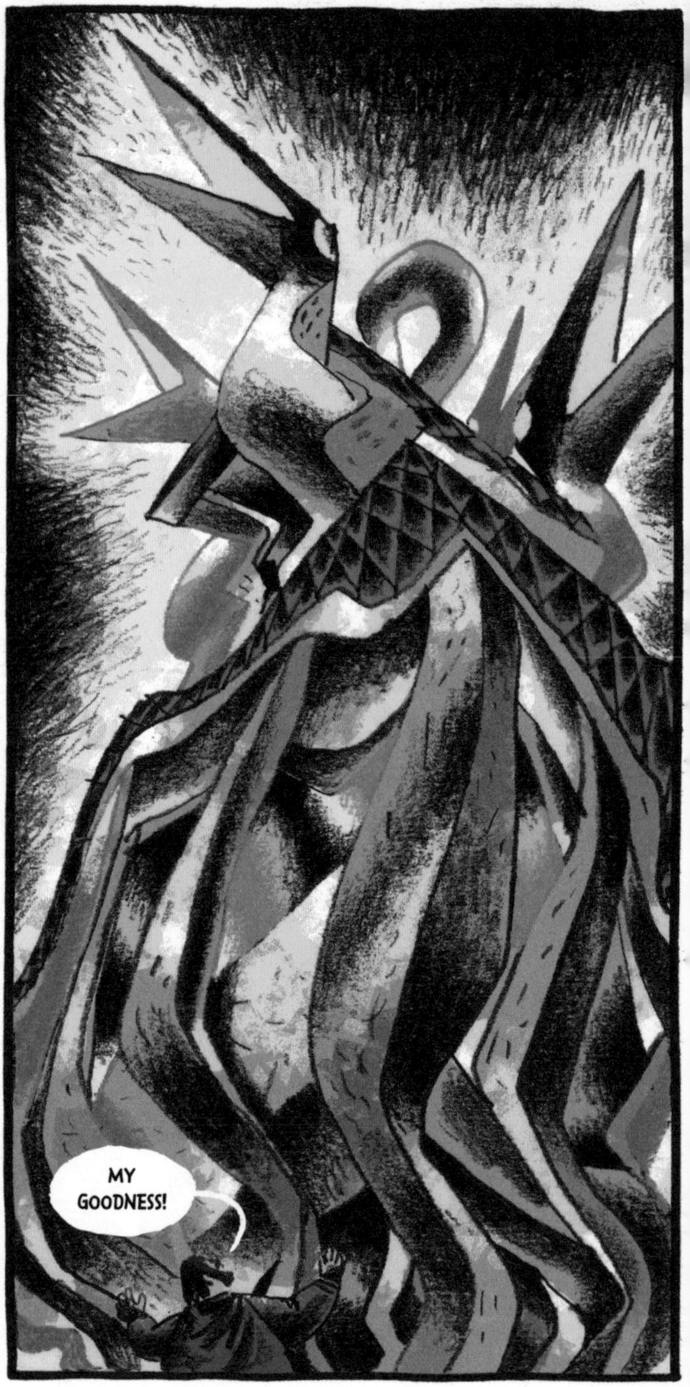
MY GOODNESS!

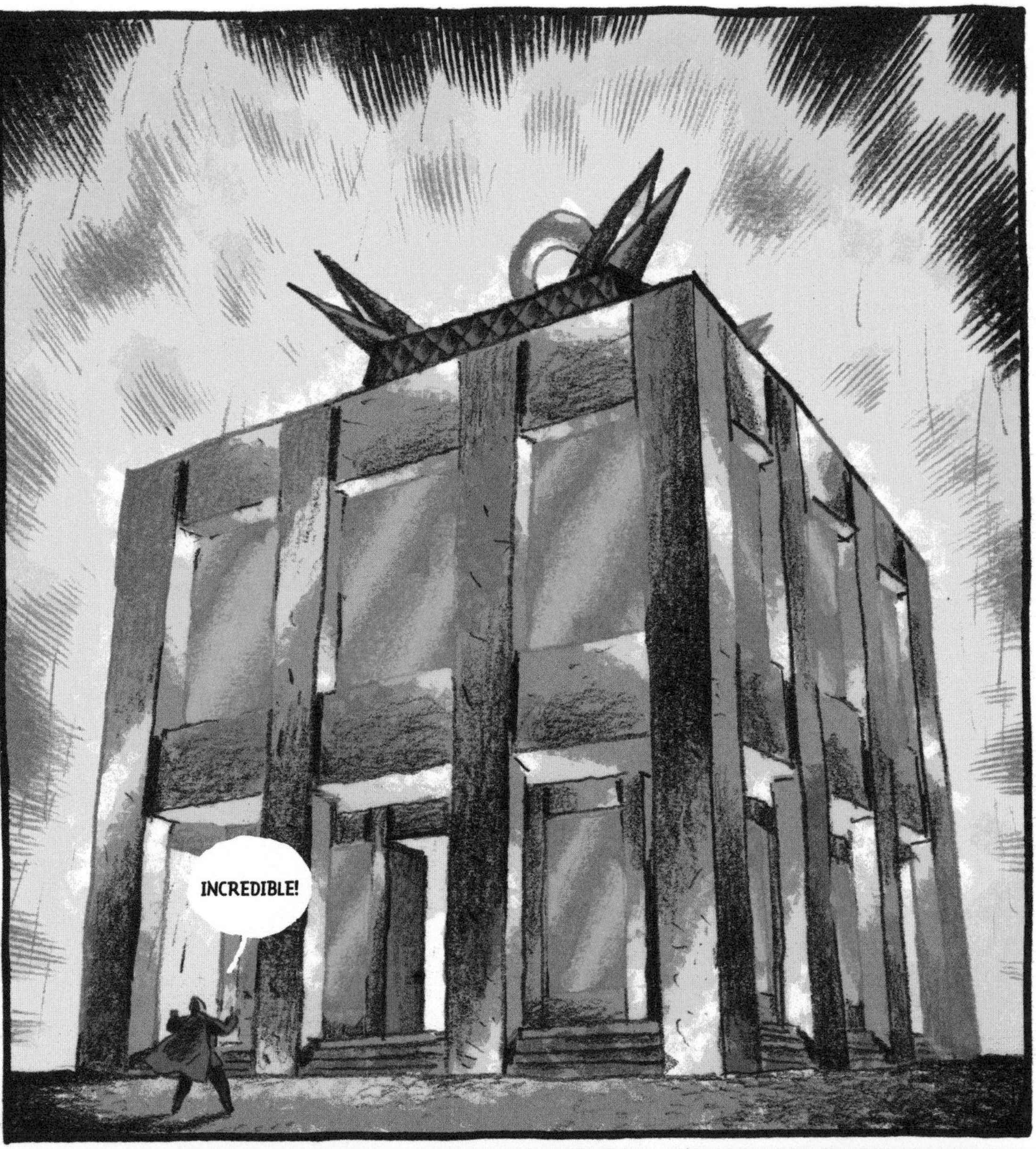
INCREDIBLE!

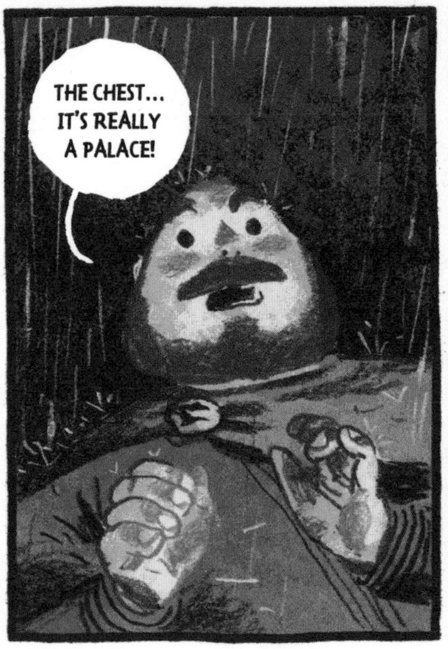
THE CHEST... IT'S REALLY A PALACE!

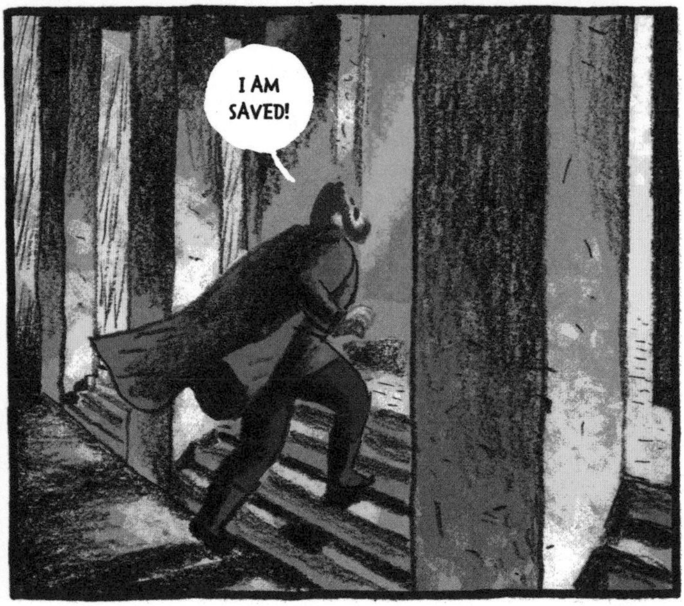
I AM SAVED!

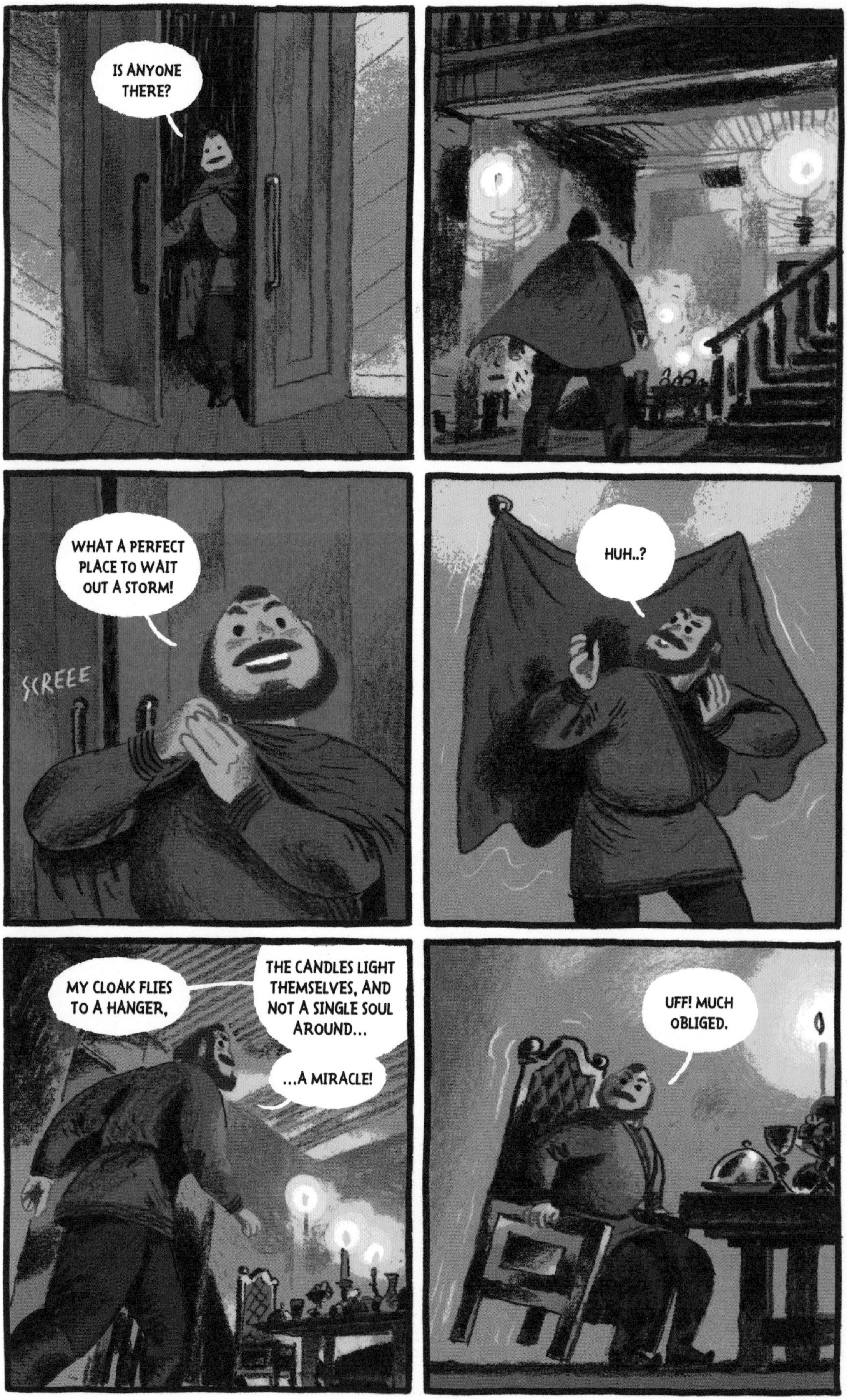
IS ANYONE THERE?
WHAT A PERFECT PLACE TO WAIT OUT A STORM!
SCREEE
HUH..?
MY CLOAK FLIES TO A HANGER,
THE CANDLES LIGHT THEMSELVES, AND NOT A SINGLE SOUL AROUND...
...A MIRACLE!
UFF! MUCH OBLIGED.

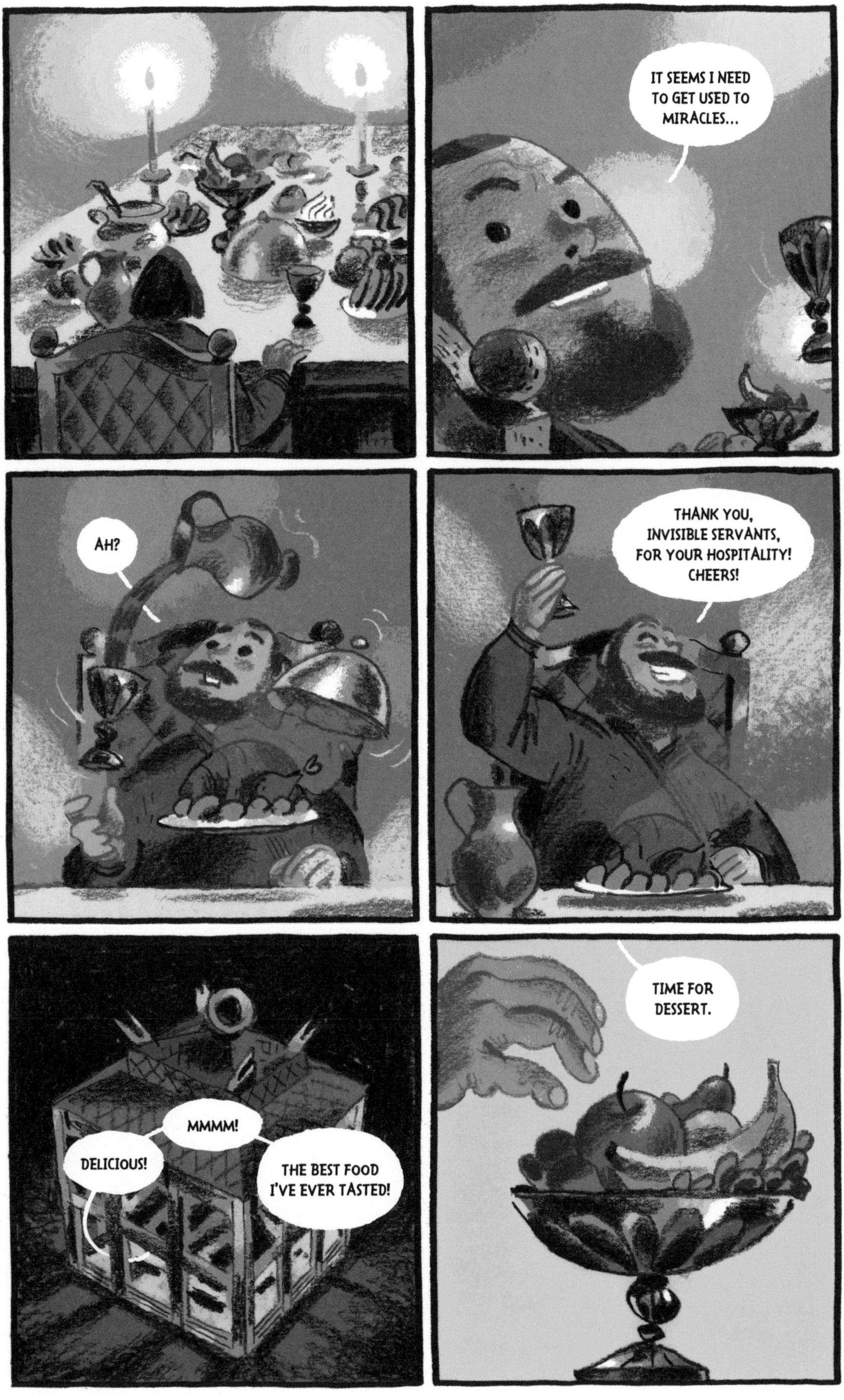
IT SEEMS I NEED TO GET USED TO MIRACLES...
AH?
THANK YOU, INVISIBLE SERVANTS, FOR YOUR HOSPITALITY! CHEERS!
MMMM!
DELICIOUS!
THE BEST FOOD I'VE EVER TASTED!
TIME FOR DESSERT.

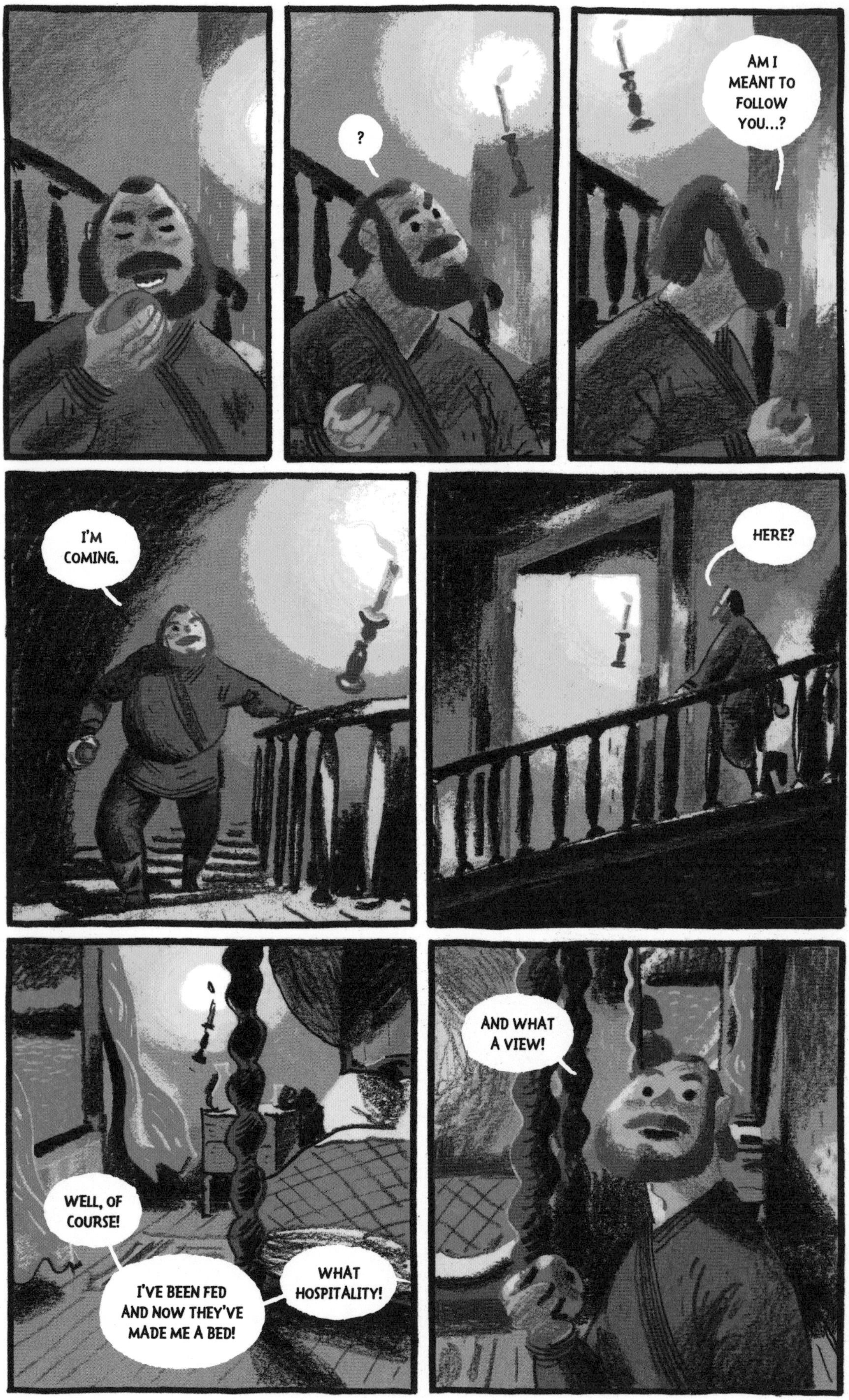
?
AM I MEANT TO FOLLOW YOU...?
I'M COMING.
HERE?
WELL, OF COURSE!
I'VE BEEN FED AND NOW THEY'VE MADE ME A BED!
WHAT HOSPITALITY!
AND WHAT A VIEW!

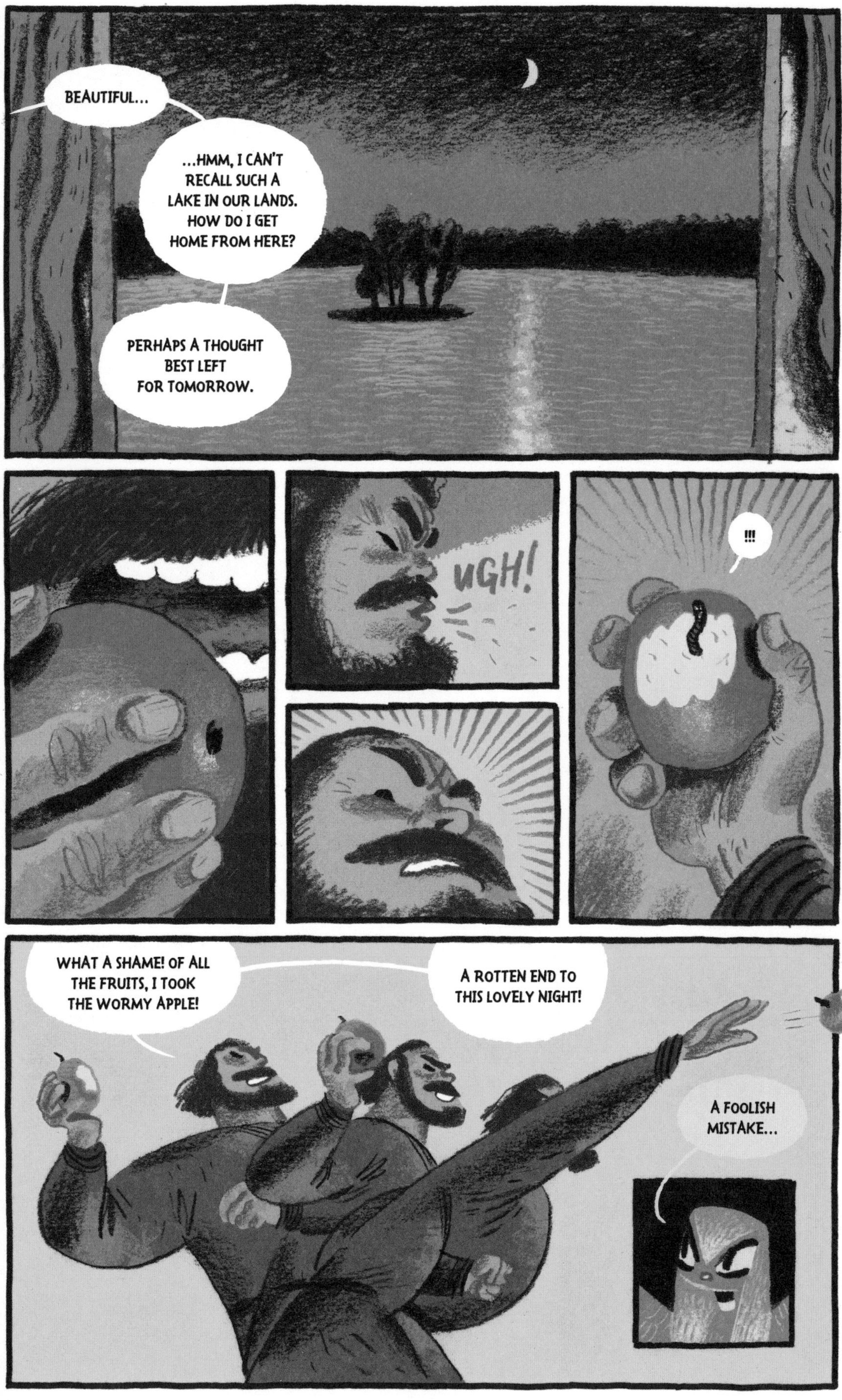
BEAUTIFUL...
...HMM, I CAN'T RECALL SUCH A LAKE IN OUR LANDS. HOW DO I GET HOME FROM HERE?
PERHAPS A THOUGHT BEST LEFT FOR TOMORROW.
UGH!
!!!
WHAT A SHAME! OF ALL THE FRUITS, I TOOK THE WORMY APPLE!
A ROTTEN END TO THIS LOVELY NIGHT!
A FOOLISH MISTAKE...

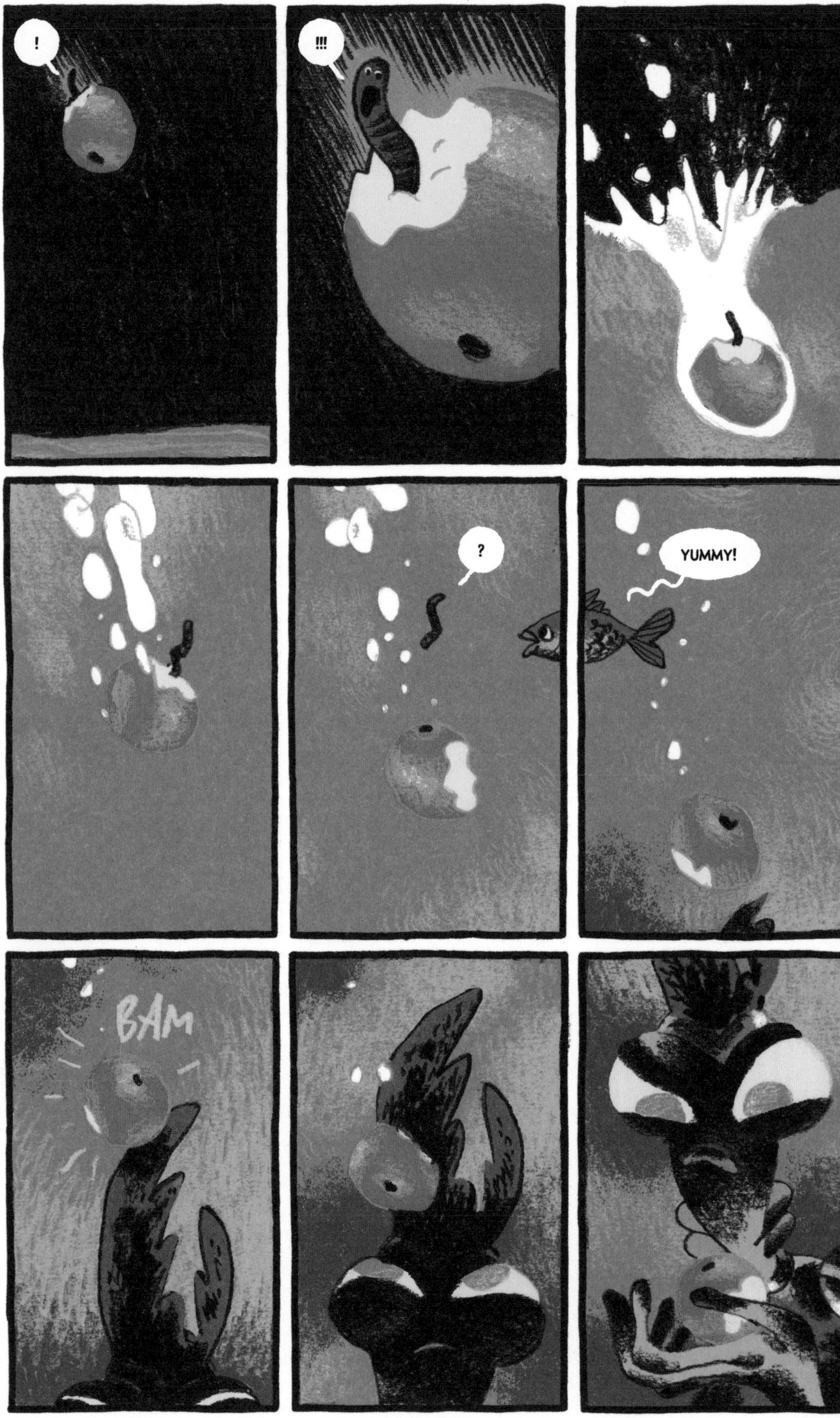
!
!!!
?
YUMMY!
BAM

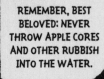
REMEMBER, BEST BELOVED: NEVER THROW APPLE CORES AND OTHER RUBBISH INTO THE WATER.

NOT ONLY DOES THIS SHOW VERY BAD MANNERS, BUT THE CONSEQUENCES MAY BE UNPREDICTABLE.

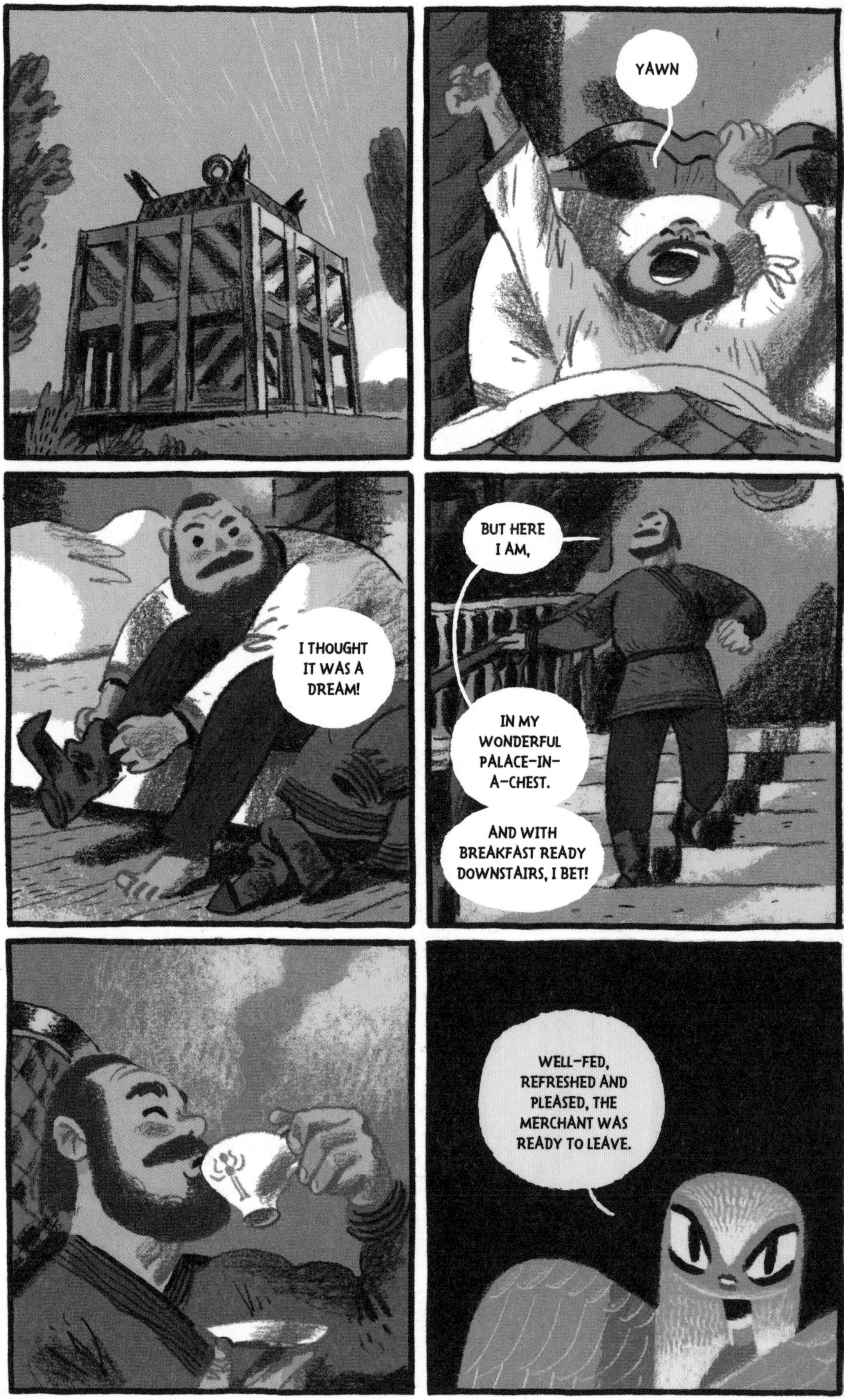
YAWN
I THOUGHT IT WAS A DREAM!
BUT HERE I AM,
IN MY WONDERFUL PALACE-IN-A-CHEST.
AND WITH BREAKFAST READY DOWNSTAIRS, I BET!
WELL-FED, REFRESHED AND PLEASED, THE MERCHANT WAS READY TO LEAVE.

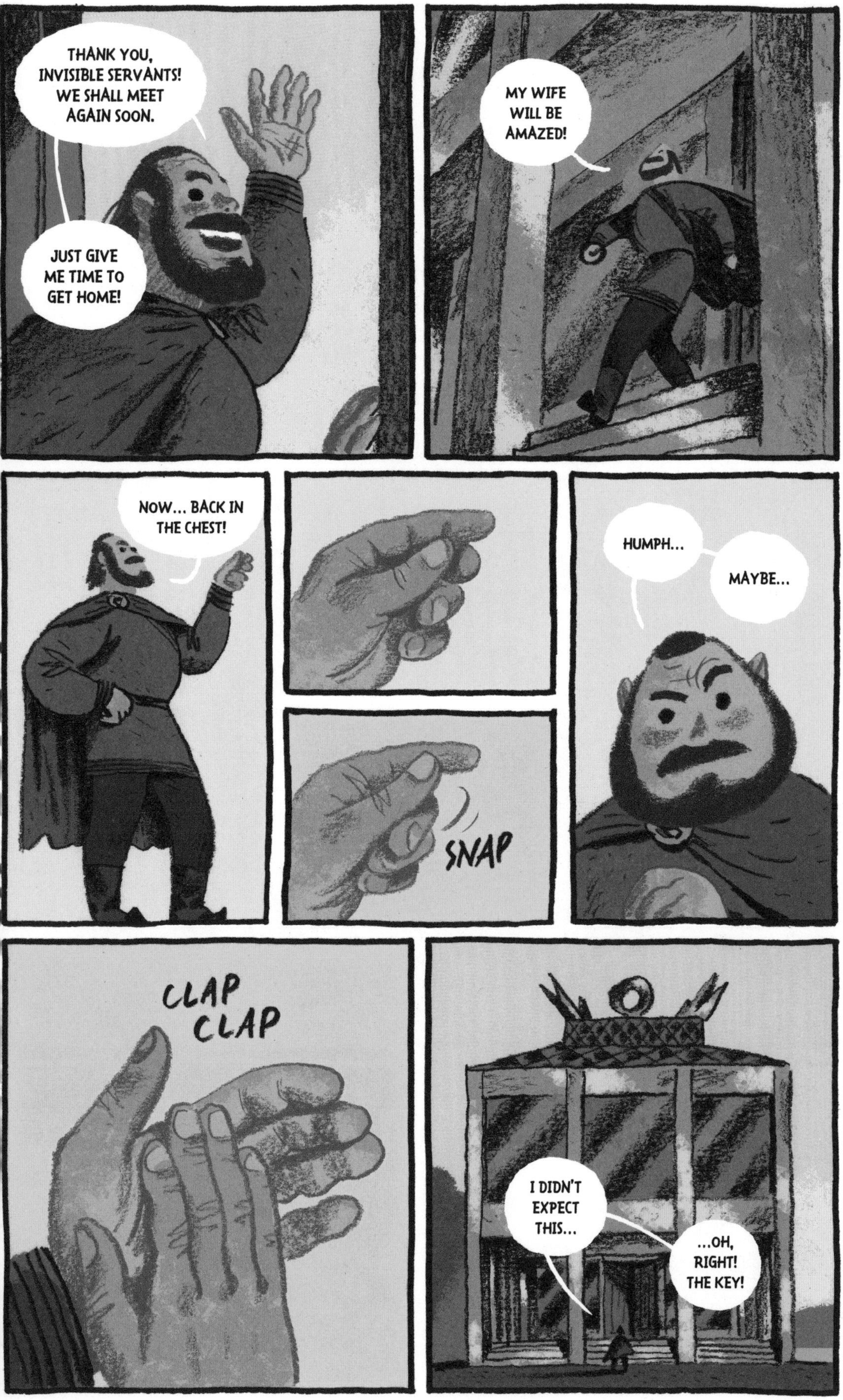
THANK YOU, INVISIBLE SERVANTS! WE SHALL MEET AGAIN SOON.
JUST GIVE ME TIME TO GET HOME!
MY WIFE WILL BE AMAZED!
NOW... BACK IN THE CHEST!
SNAP
HUMPH...
MAYBE...
CLAP CLAP
I DIDN'T EXPECT THIS...
...OH, RIGHT! THE KEY!

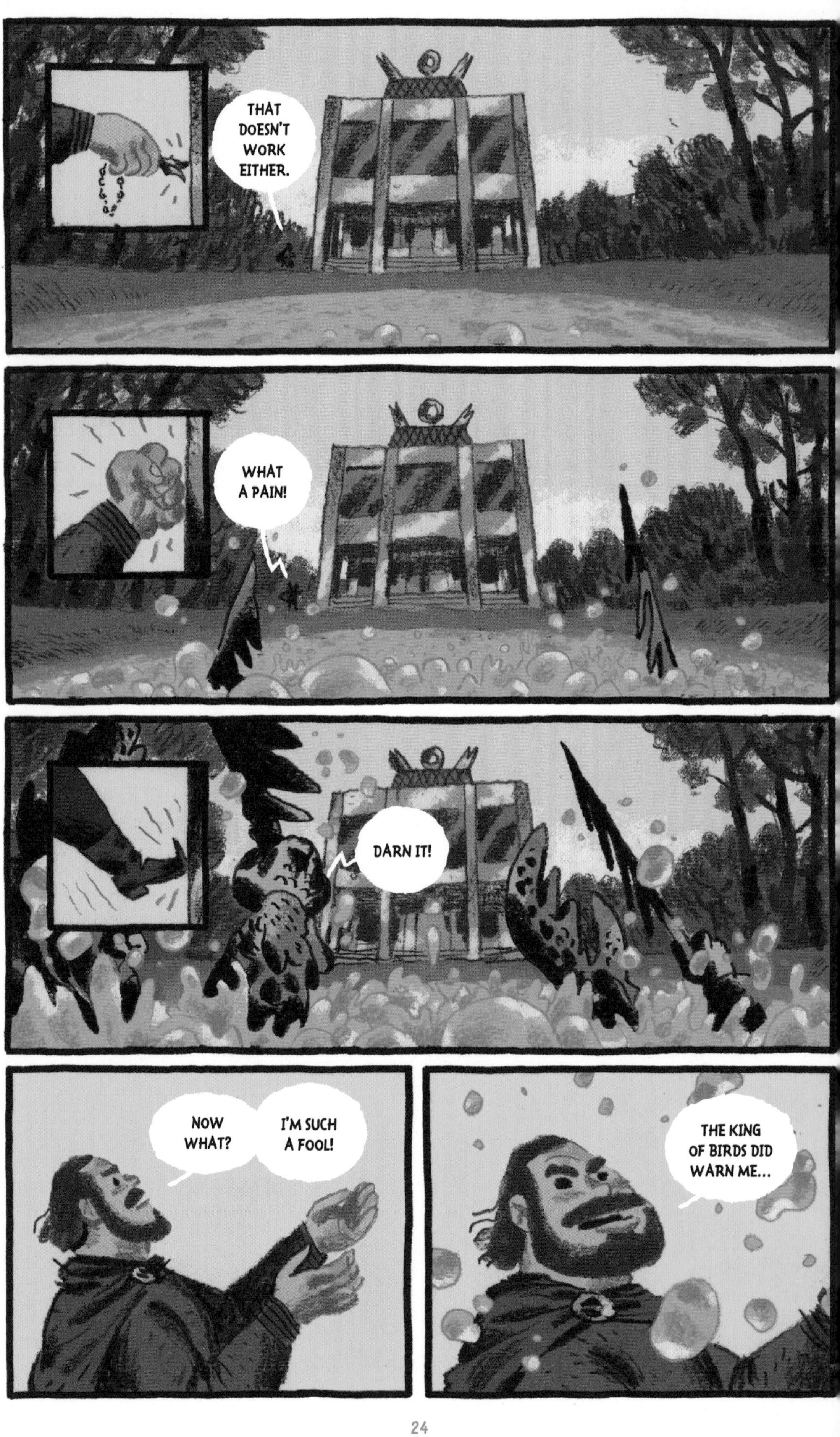
THAT DOESN'T WORK EITHER.
WHAT A PAIN!
DARN IT!
NOW WHAT?
I'M SUCH A FOOL!
THE KING OF BIRDS DID WARN ME...

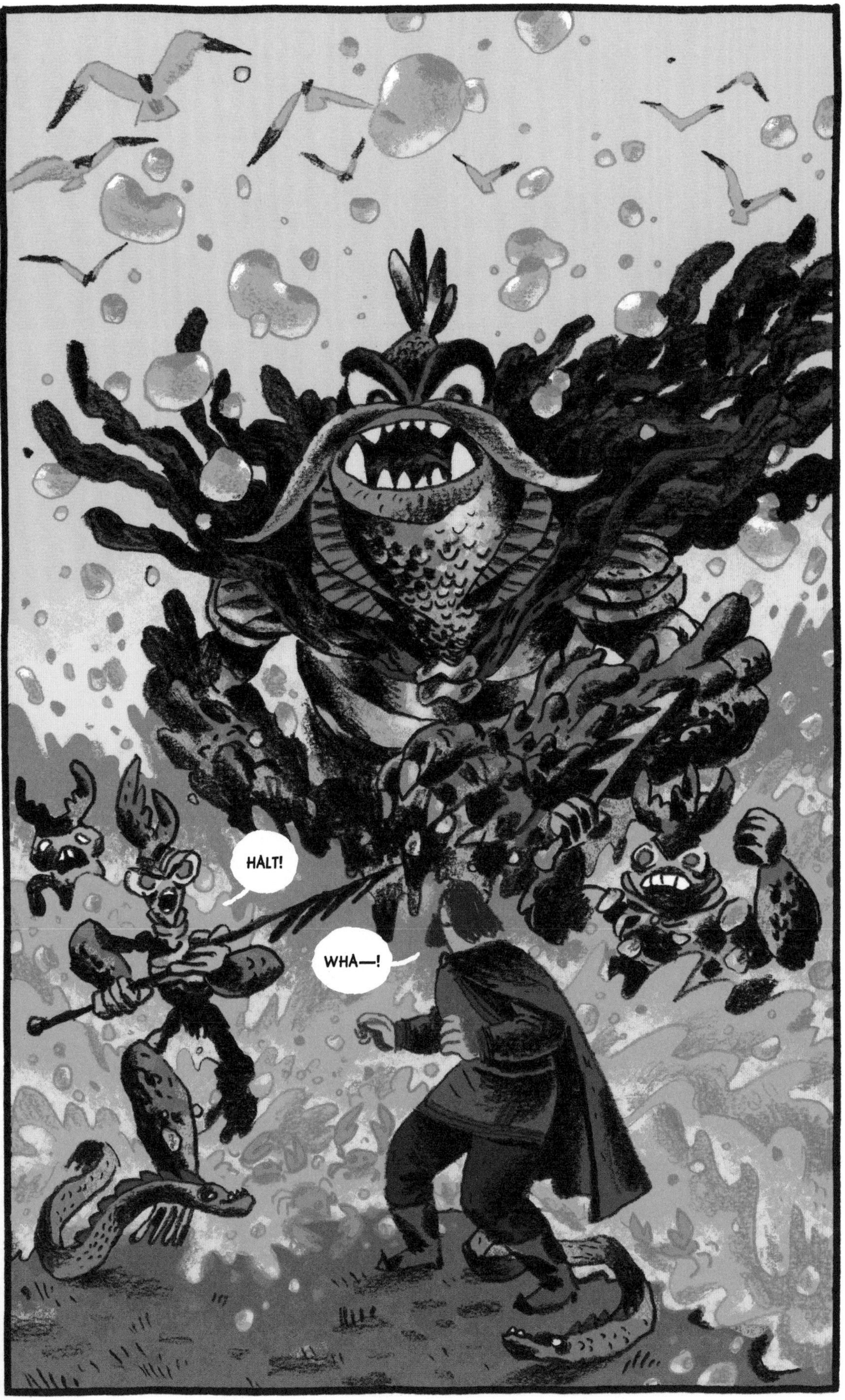
HALT!
WHA—!

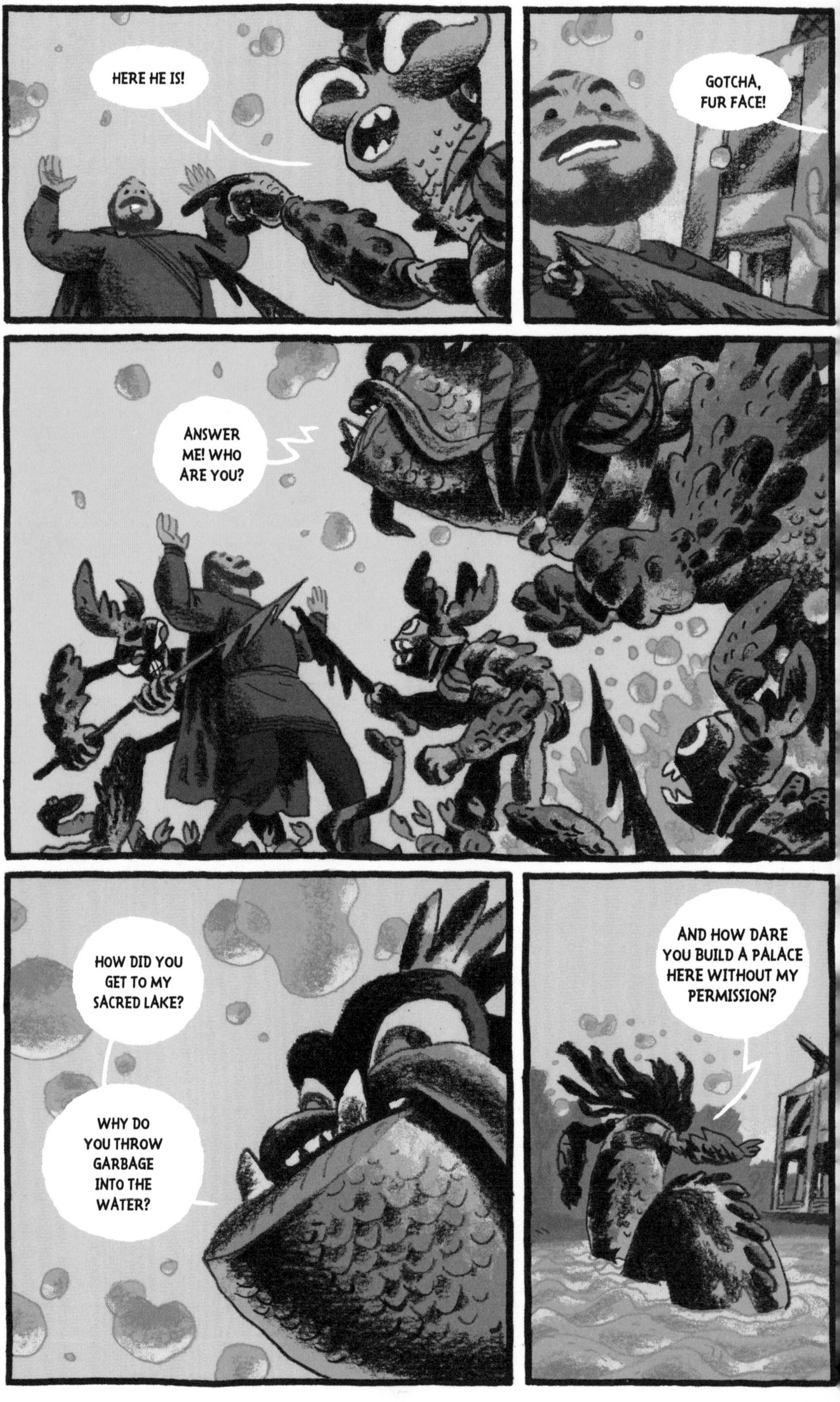
HERE HE IS!
GOTCHA, FUR FACE!
ANSWER ME! WHO ARE YOU?
HOW DID YOU GET TO MY SACRED LAKE?
WHY DO YOU THROW GARBAGE INTO THE WATER?
AND HOW DARE YOU BUILD A PALACE HERE WITHOUT MY PERMISSION?

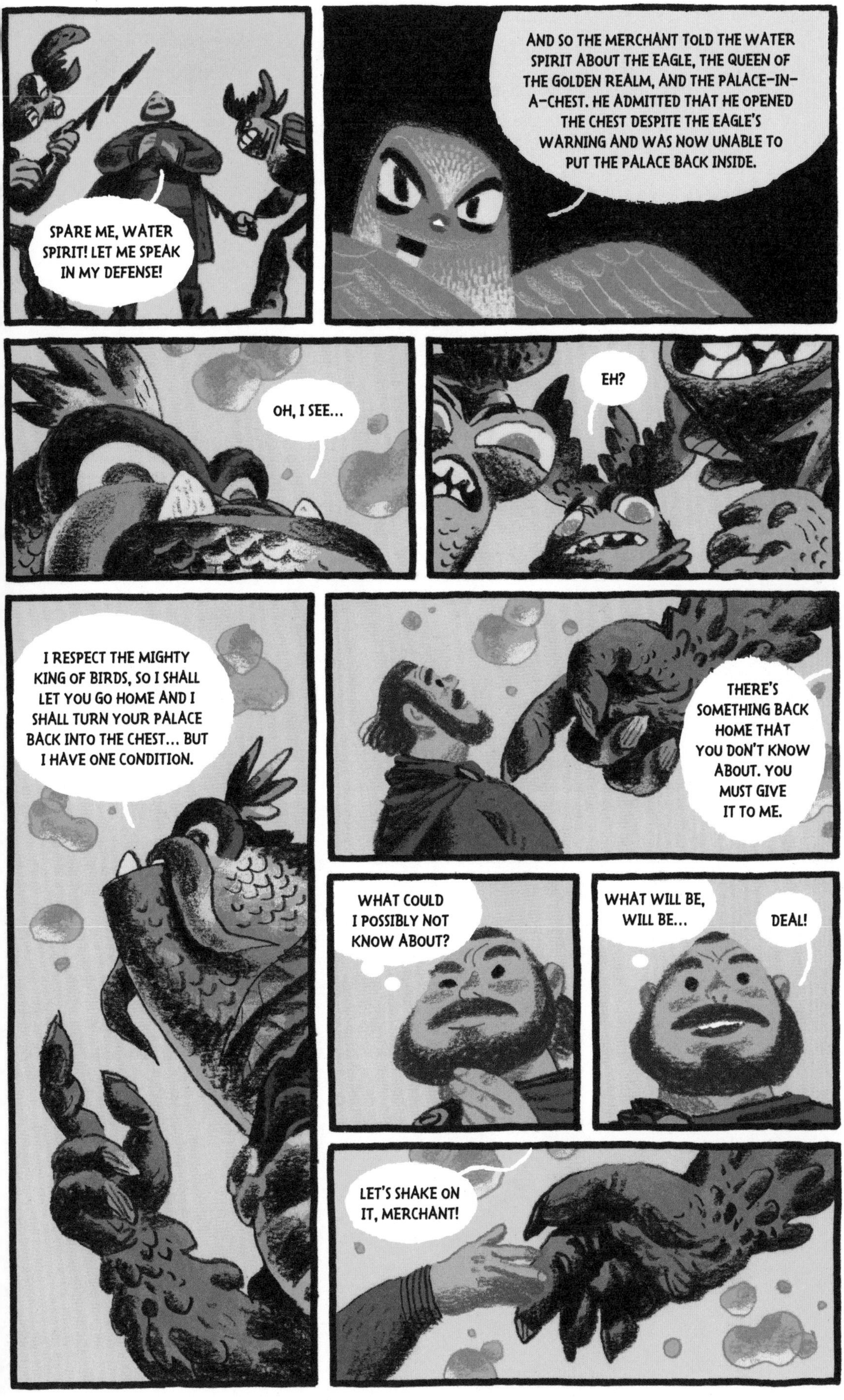
SPARE ME, WATER SPIRIT! LET ME SPEAK IN MY DEFENSE!
AND SO THE MERCHANT TOLD THE WATER SPIRIT ABOUT THE EAGLE, THE QUEEN OF THE GOLDEN REALM, AND THE PALACE-IN-A-CHEST. HE ADMITTED THAT HE OPENED THE CHEST DESPITE THE EAGLE'S WARNING AND WAS NOW UNABLE TO PUT THE PALACE BACK INSIDE.
OH, I SEE...
EH?
I RESPECT THE MIGHTY KING OF BIRDS, SO I SHALL LET YOU GO HOME AND I SHALL TURN YOUR PALACE BACK INTO THE CHEST... BUT I HAVE ONE CONDITION.
THERE'S SOMETHING BACK HOME THAT YOU DON'T KNOW ABOUT. YOU MUST GIVE IT TO ME.
WHAT COULD I POSSIBLY NOT KNOW ABOUT?
WHAT WILL BE, WILL BE...
DEAL!
LET'S SHAKE ON IT, MERCHANT!

NOW WHAT HAVE WE GOT HERE...

STAY OUT OF THIS, SHAGGY! OR I'LL GRIND YOU INTO DUST!

WHO IS THIS "SHAGGY" THREATENED BY THE WATER SPIRIT? ALL WILL BE REVEALED IN DUE TIME...

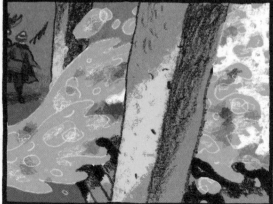

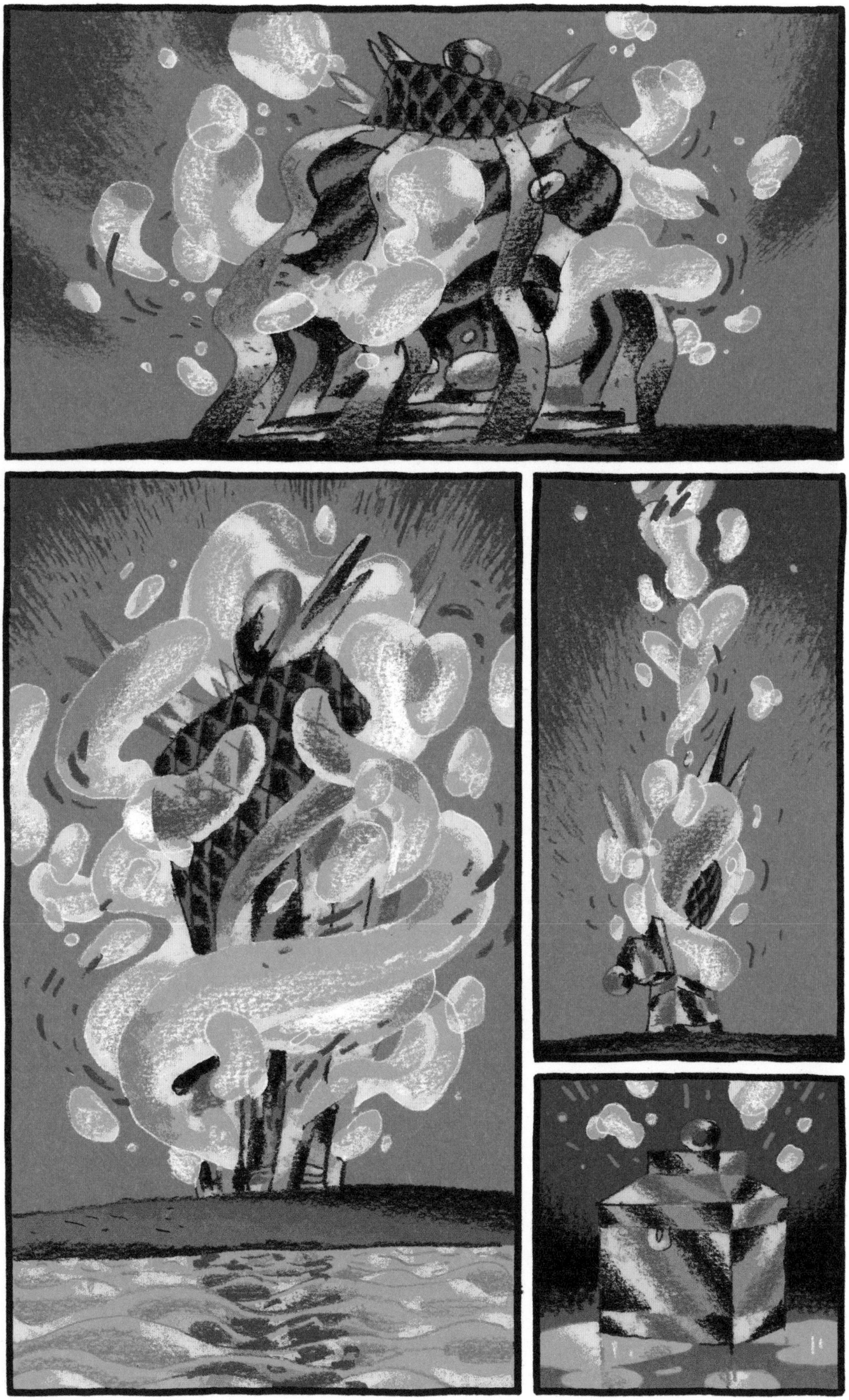

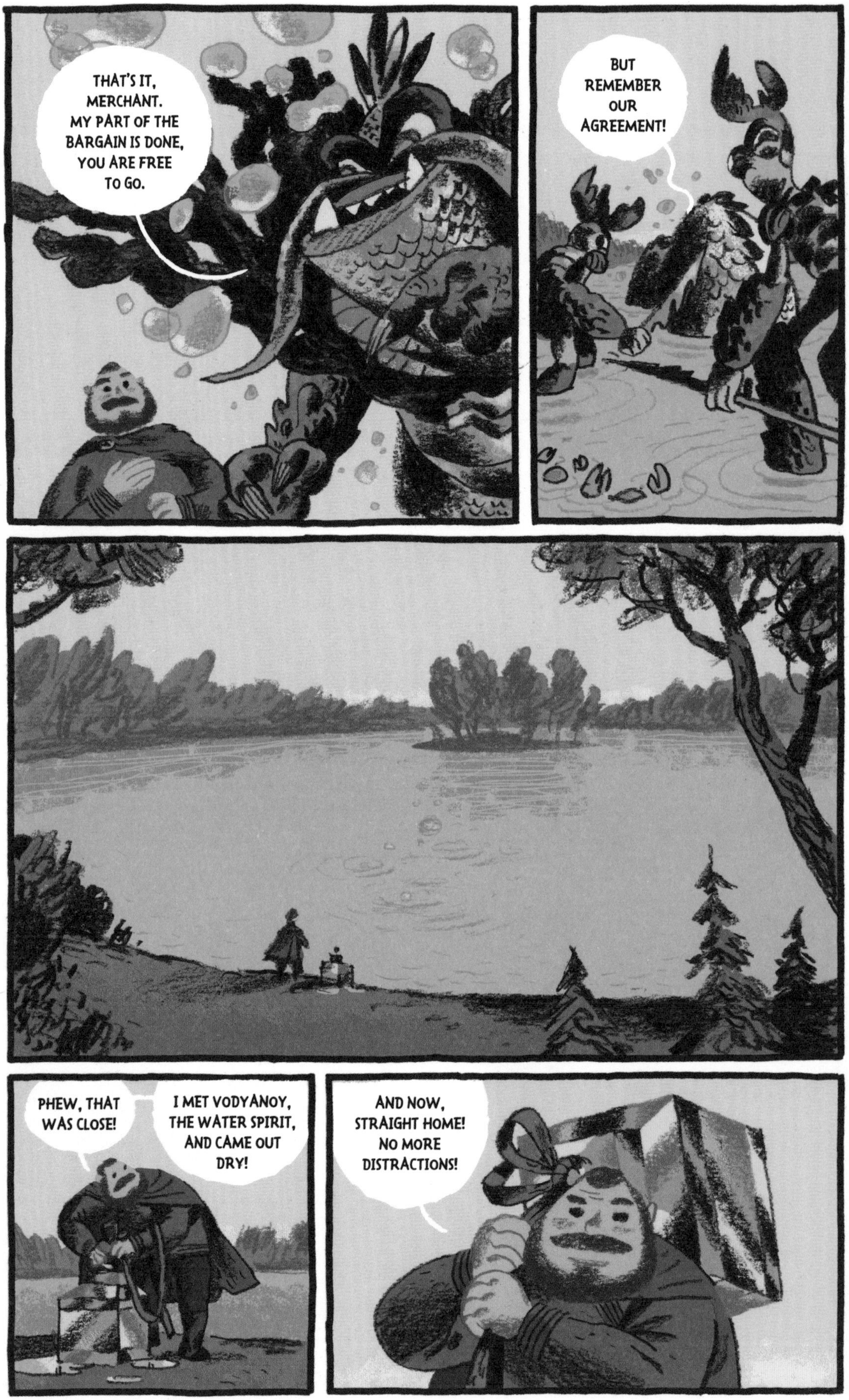
THAT'S IT, MERCHANT. MY PART OF THE BARGAIN IS DONE, YOU ARE FREE TO GO.
BUT REMEMBER OUR AGREEMENT!
PHEW, THAT WAS CLOSE!
I MET VODYANOY, THE WATER SPIRIT, AND CAME OUT DRY!
AND NOW, STRAIGHT HOME! NO MORE DISTRACTIONS!

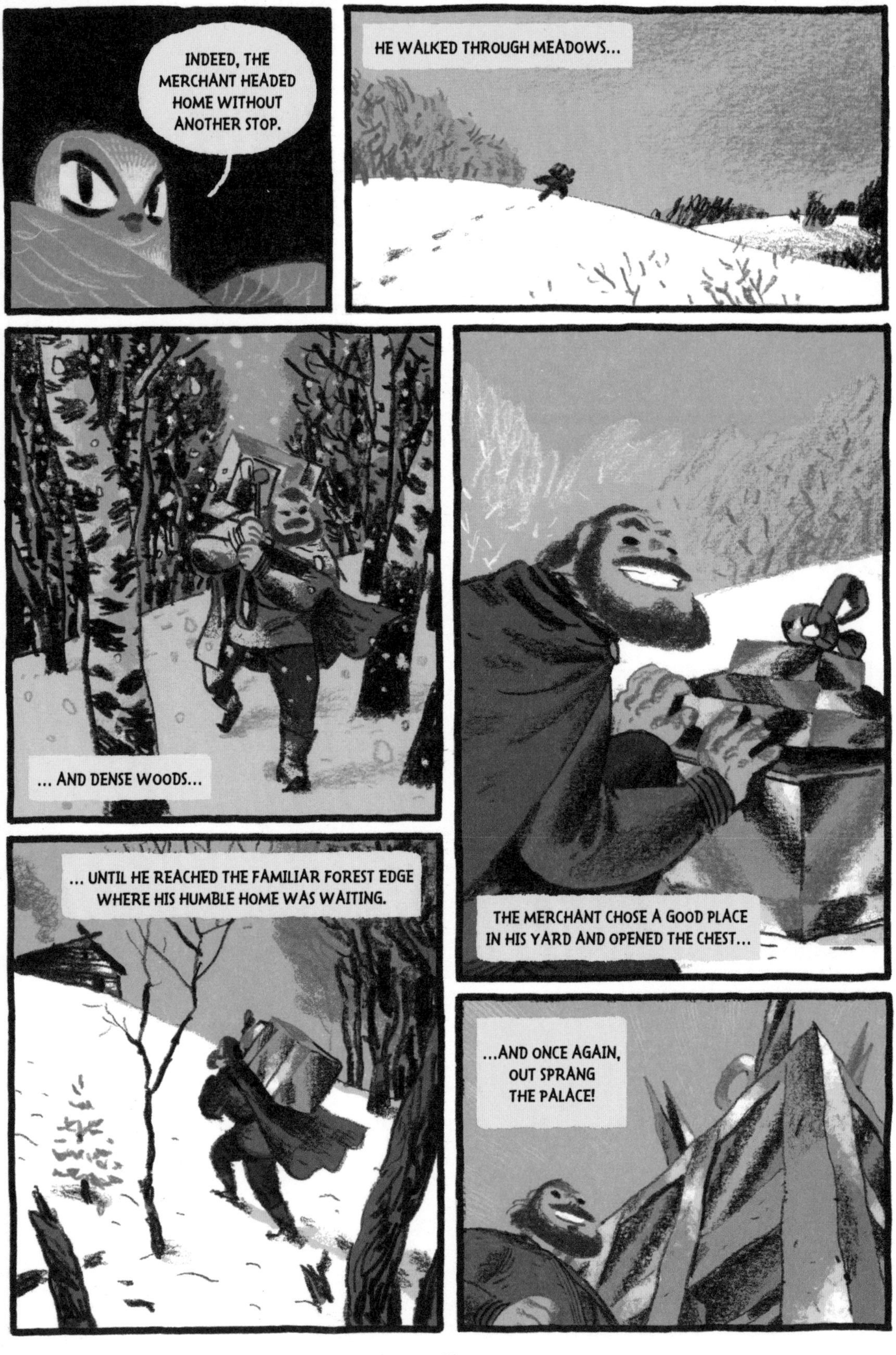
INDEED, THE MERCHANT HEADED HOME WITHOUT ANOTHER STOP.
HE WALKED THROUGH MEADOWS...
... AND DENSE WOODS...
THE MERCHANT CHOSE A GOOD PLACE IN HIS YARD AND OPENED THE CHEST...
... UNTIL HE REACHED THE FAMILIAR FOREST EDGE WHERE HIS HUMBLE HOME WAS WAITING.
...AND ONCE AGAIN, OUT SPRANG THE PALACE!

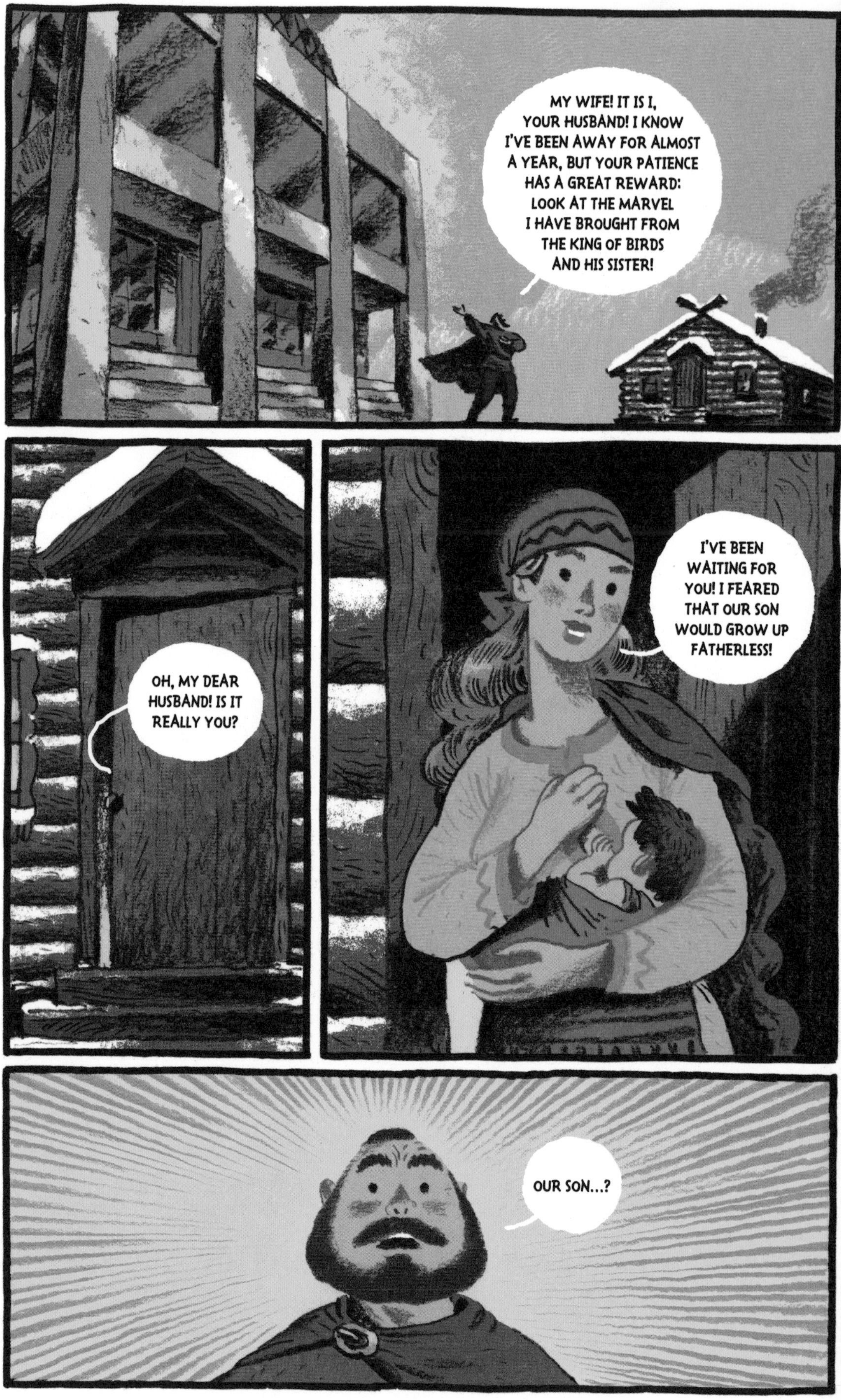
MY WIFE! IT IS I, YOUR HUSBAND! I KNOW I'VE BEEN AWAY FOR ALMOST A YEAR, BUT YOUR PATIENCE HAS A GREAT REWARD: LOOK AT THE MARVEL I HAVE BROUGHT FROM THE KING OF BIRDS AND HIS SISTER!
OH, MY DEAR HUSBAND! IS IT REALLY YOU?
I'VE BEEN WAITING FOR YOU! I FEARED THAT OUR SON WOULD GROW UP FATHERLESS!
OUR SON...?

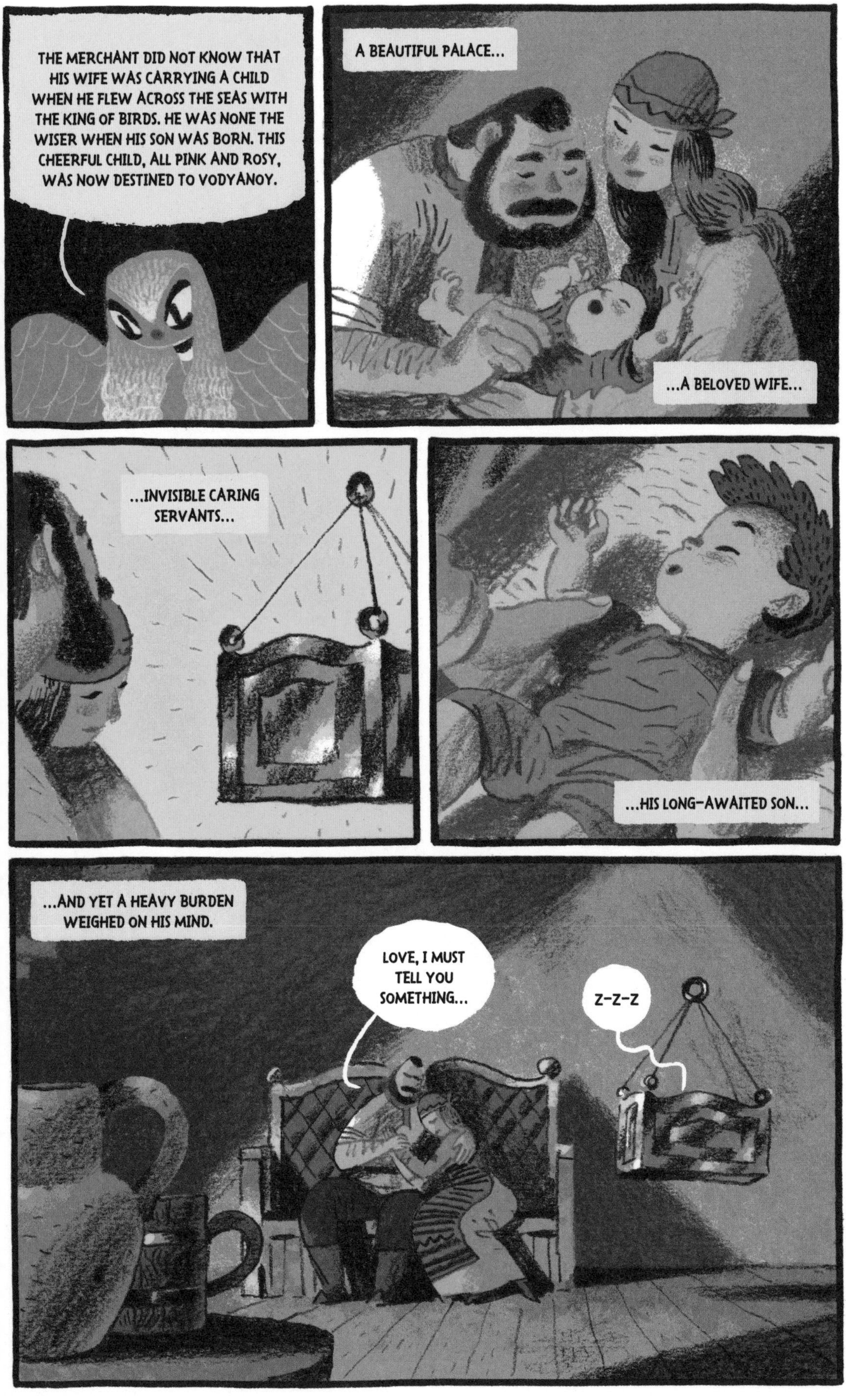

THE MERCHANT DID NOT KNOW THAT HIS WIFE WAS CARRYING A CHILD WHEN HE FLEW ACROSS THE SEAS WITH THE KING OF BIRDS. HE WAS NONE THE WISER WHEN HIS SON WAS BORN. THIS CHEERFUL CHILD, ALL PINK AND ROSY, WAS NOW DESTINED TO VODYANOY.
A BEAUTIFUL PALACE...
...A BELOVED WIFE...
...INVISIBLE CARING SERVANTS...
...HIS LONG-AWAITED SON...
...AND YET A HEAVY BURDEN WEIGHED ON HIS MIND.
LOVE, I MUST TELL YOU SOMETHING...
Z-Z-Z

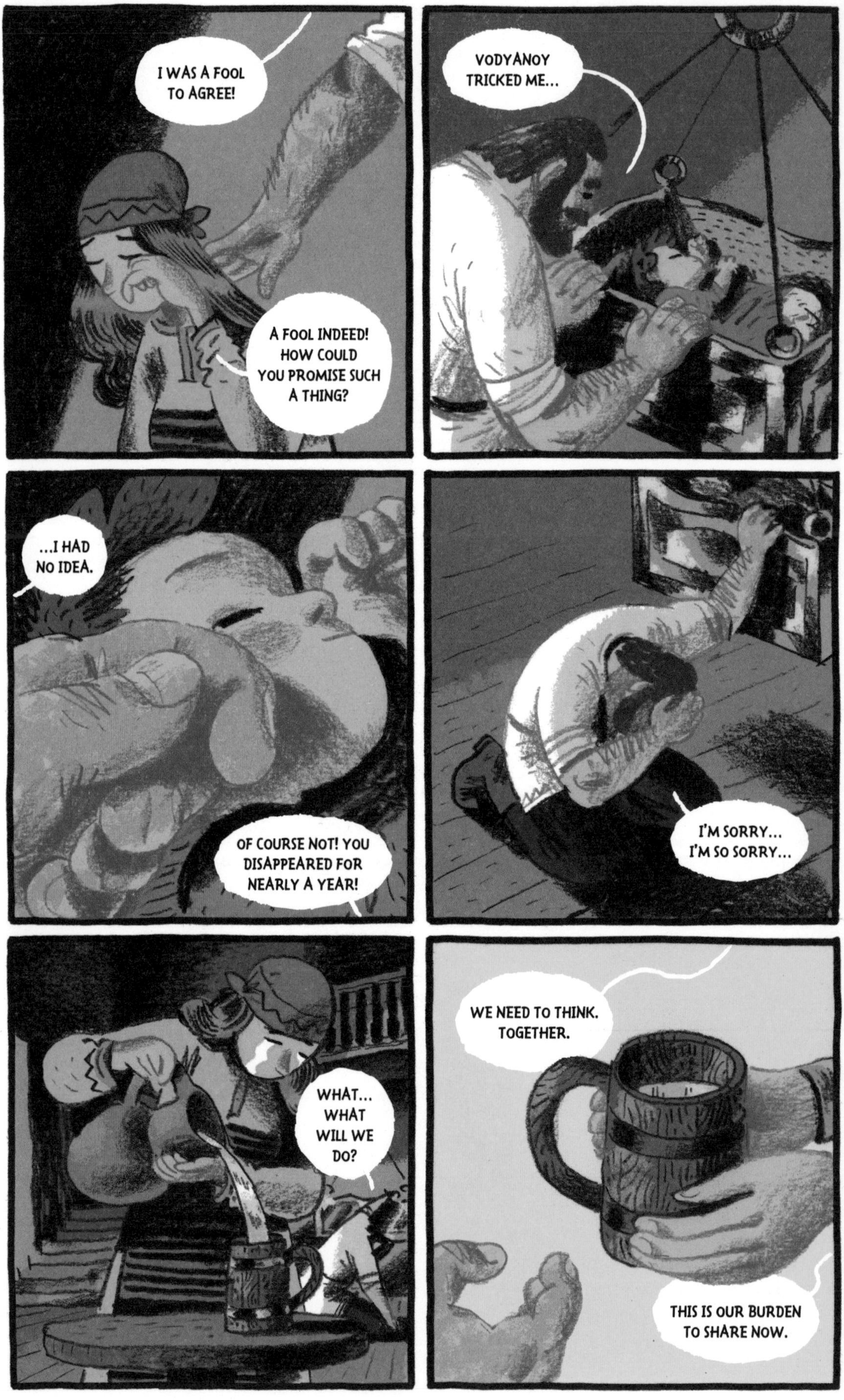
I WAS A FOOL TO AGREE!
A FOOL INDEED! HOW COULD YOU PROMISE SUCH A THING?
VODYANOY TRICKED ME...
...I HAD NO IDEA.
OF COURSE NOT! YOU DISAPPEARED FOR NEARLY A YEAR!
I'M SORRY... I'M SO SORRY...
WHAT... WHAT WILL WE DO?
WE NEED TO THINK. TOGETHER.
THIS IS OUR BURDEN TO SHARE NOW.

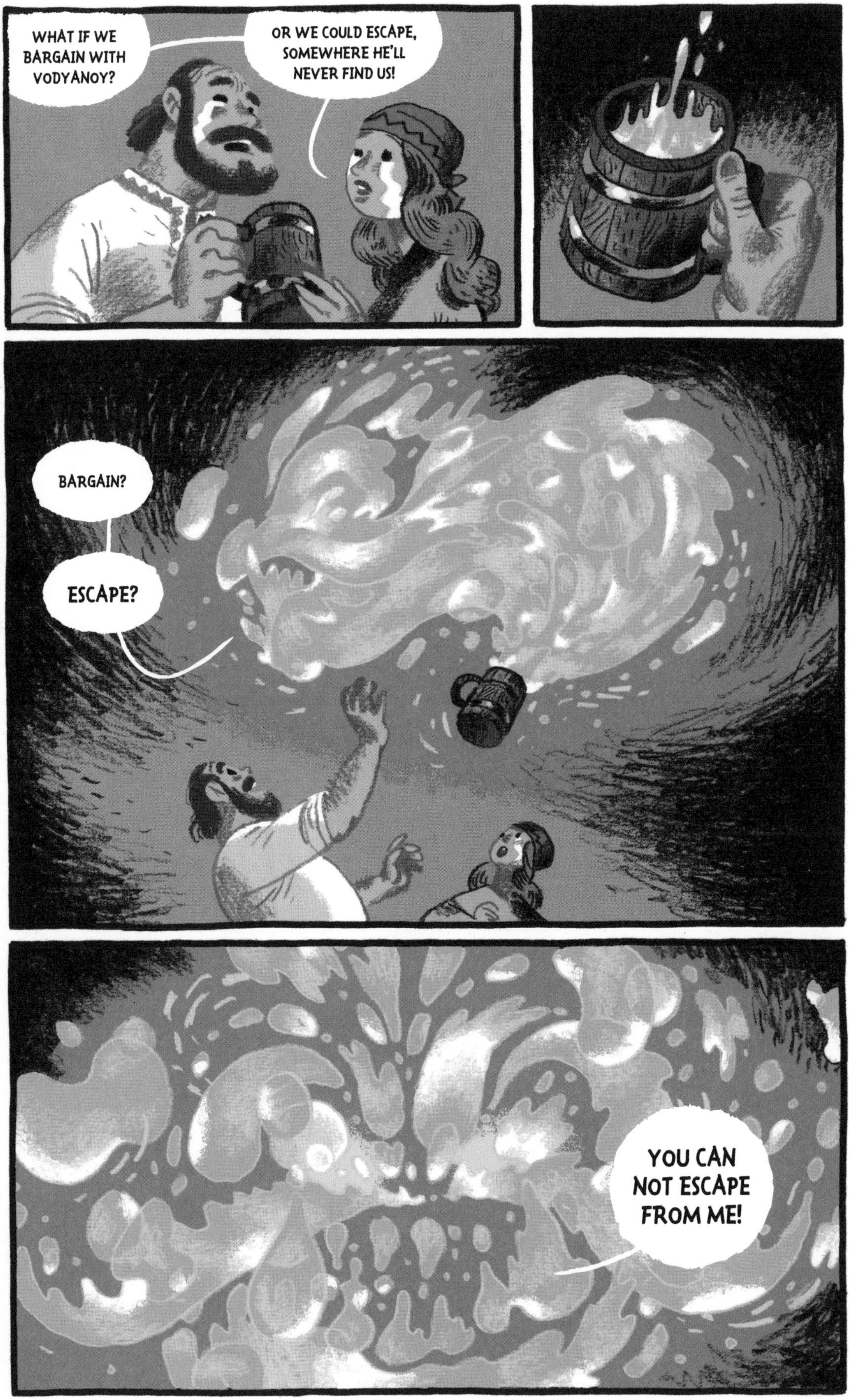
WHAT IF WE BARGAIN WITH VODYANOY?
OR WE COULD ESCAPE, SOMEWHERE HE'LL NEVER FIND US!
BARGAIN?
ESCAPE?
YOU CAN NOT ESCAPE FROM ME!

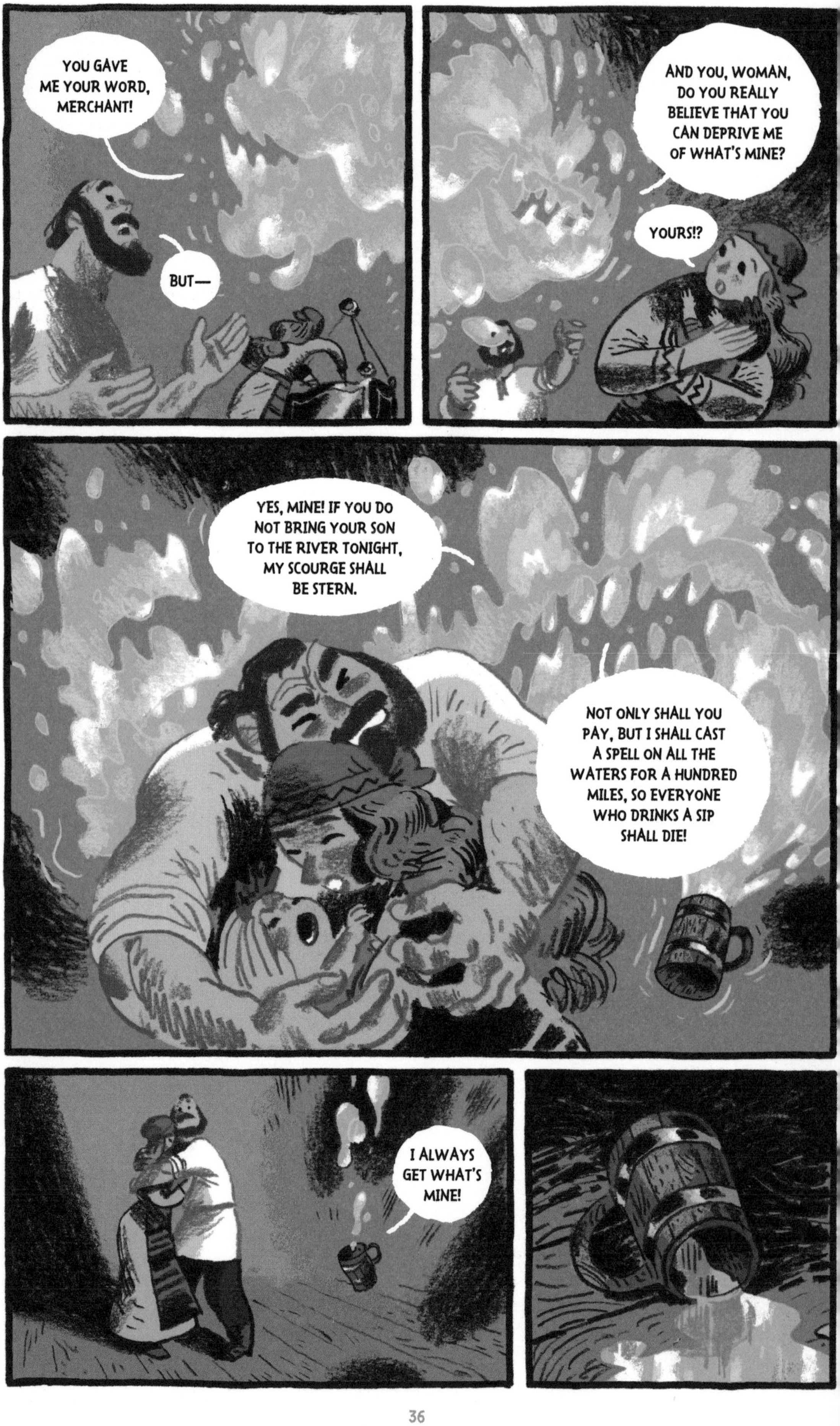
YOU GAVE ME YOUR WORD, MERCHANT!
BUT—
AND YOU, WOMAN, DO YOU REALLY BELIEVE THAT YOU CAN DEPRIVE ME OF WHAT'S MINE?
YOURS!?
YES, MINE! IF YOU DO NOT BRING YOUR SON TO THE RIVER TONIGHT, MY SCOURGE SHALL BE STERN.
NOT ONLY SHALL YOU PAY, BUT I SHALL CAST A SPELL ON ALL THE WATERS FOR A HUNDRED MILES, SO EVERYONE WHO DRINKS A SIP SHALL DIE!
I ALWAYS GET WHAT'S MINE!

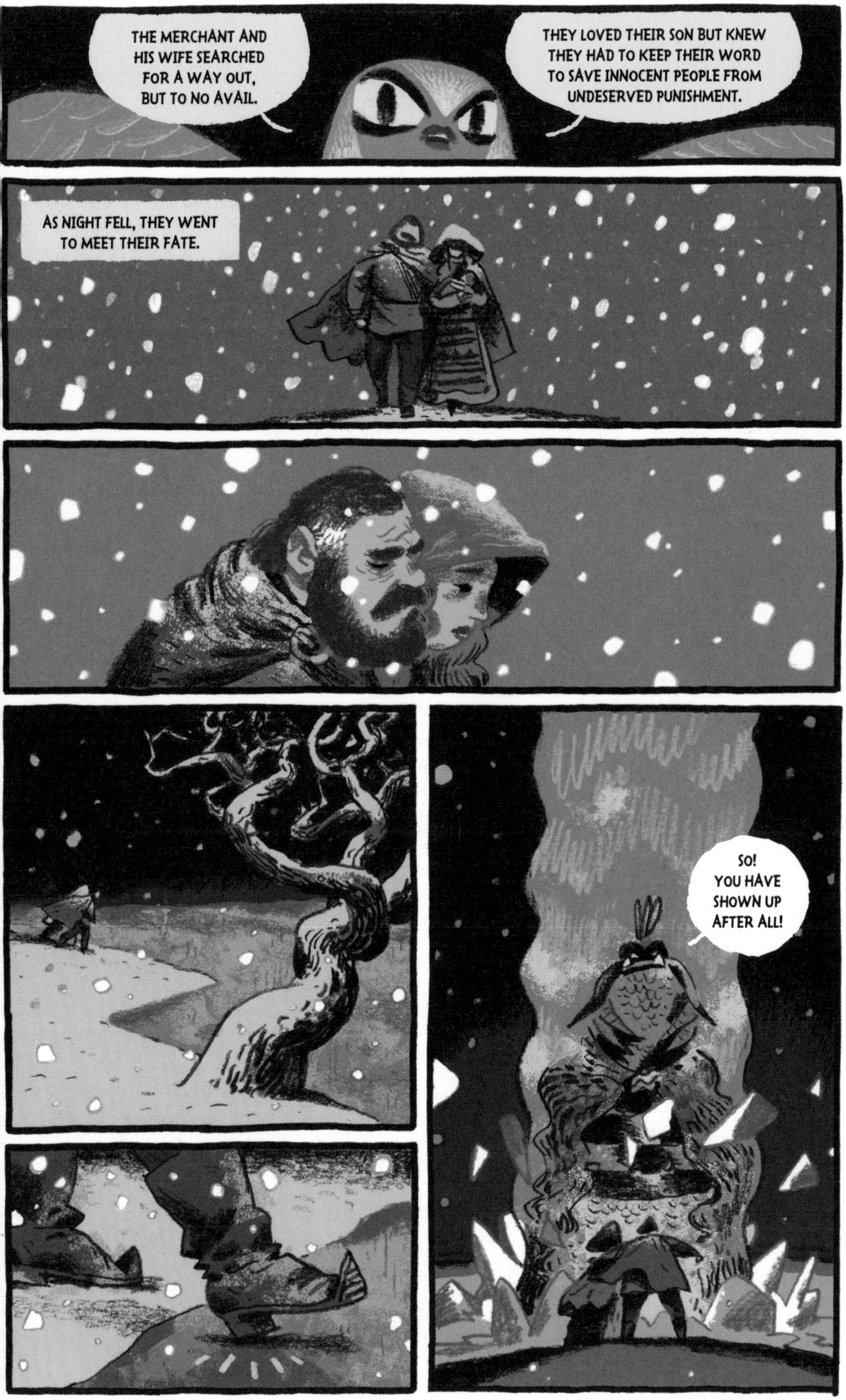
THE MERCHANT AND HIS WIFE SEARCHED FOR A WAY OUT, BUT TO NO AVAIL.
THEY LOVED THEIR SON BUT KNEW THEY HAD TO KEEP THEIR WORD TO SAVE INNOCENT PEOPLE FROM UNDESERVED PUNISHMENT.
AS NIGHT FELL, THEY WENT TO MEET THEIR FATE.
SO! YOU HAVE SHOWN UP AFTER ALL!

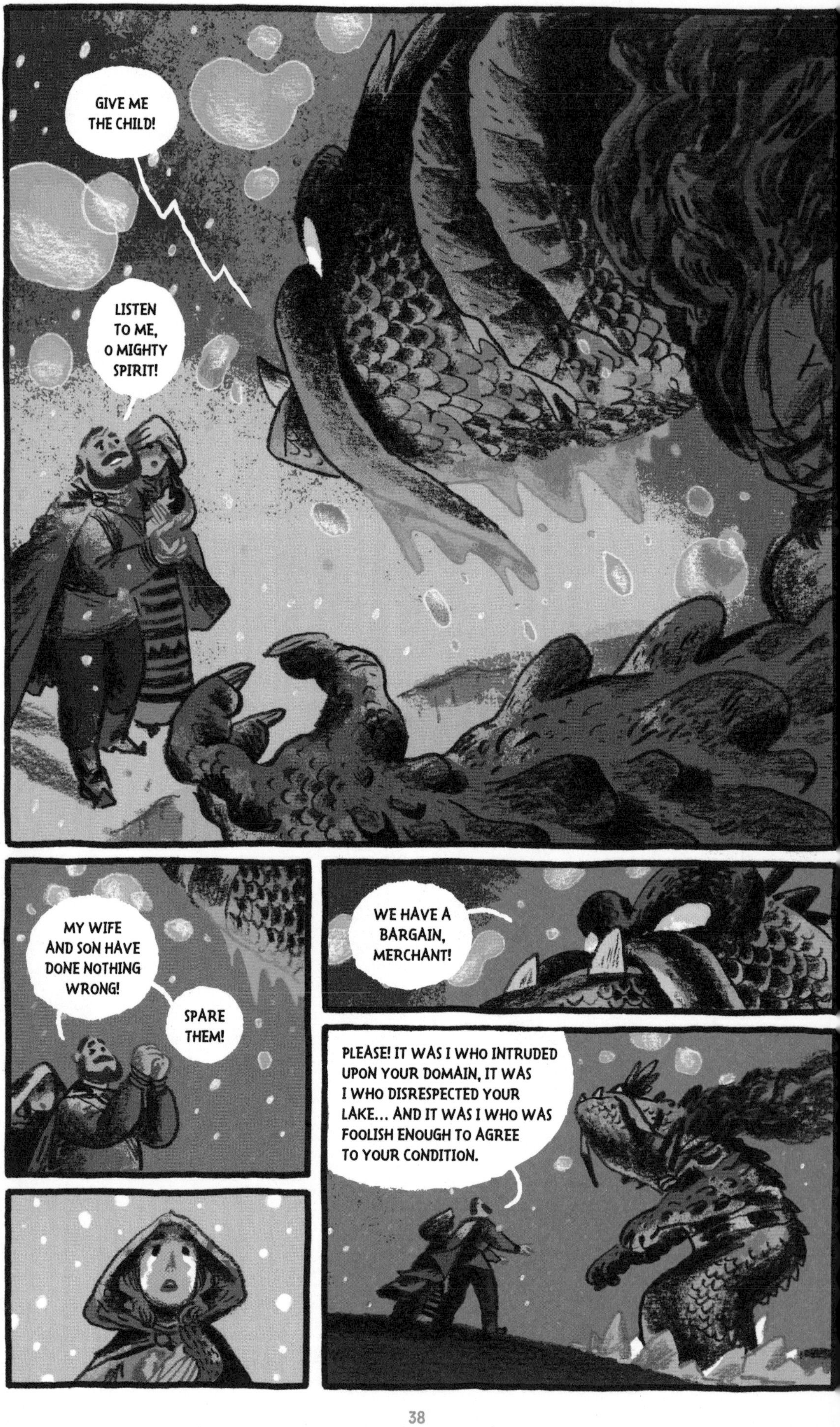
GIVE ME THE CHILD!
LISTEN TO ME, O MIGHTY SPIRIT!
MY WIFE AND SON HAVE DONE NOTHING WRONG!
SPARE THEM!
WE HAVE A BARGAIN, MERCHANT!
PLEASE! IT WAS I WHO INTRUDED UPON YOUR DOMAIN, IT WAS I WHO DISRESPECTED YOUR LAKE... AND IT WAS I WHO WAS FOOLISH ENOUGH TO AGREE TO YOUR CONDITION.

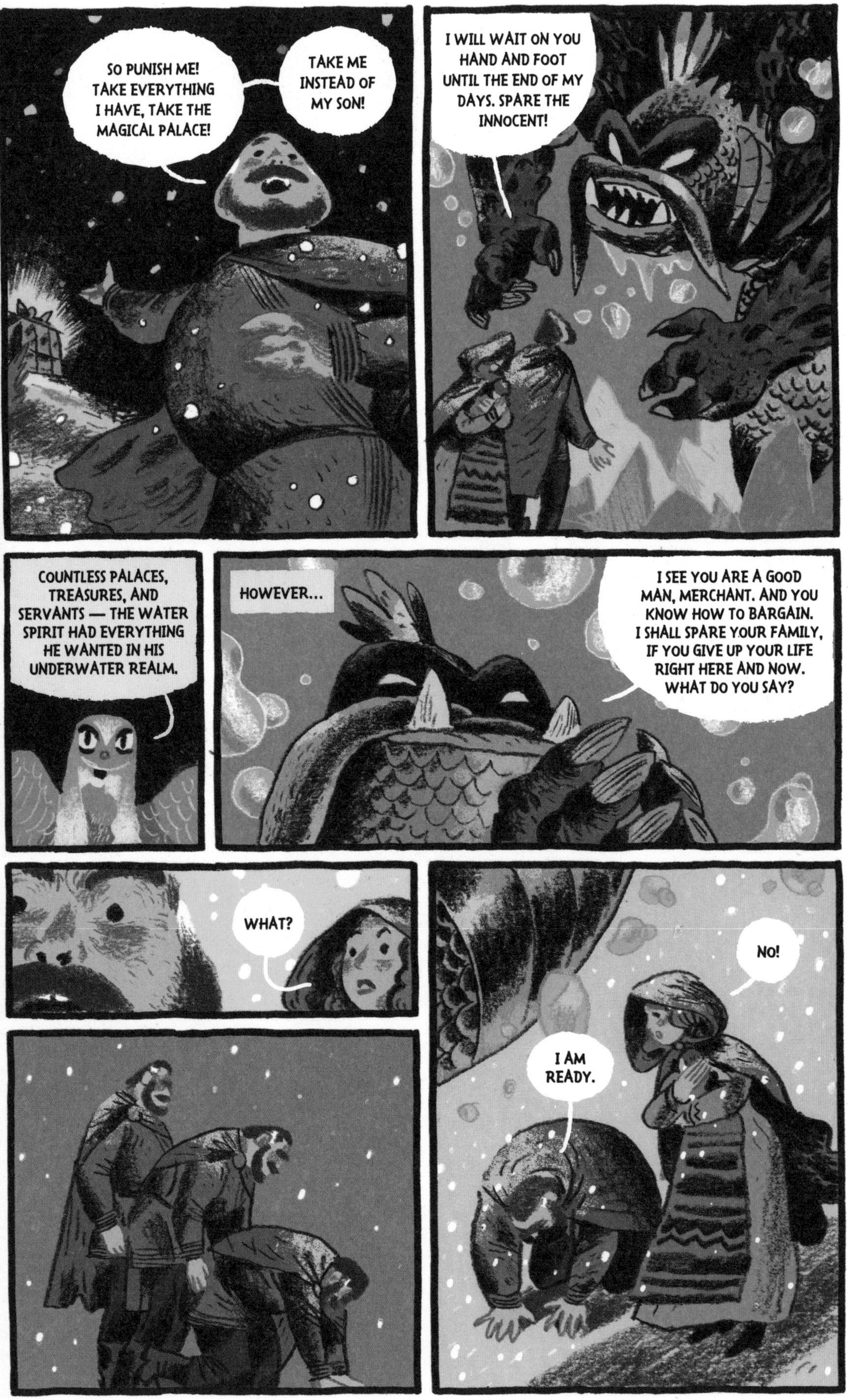
SO PUNISH ME! TAKE EVERYTHING I HAVE, TAKE THE MAGICAL PALACE!
TAKE ME INSTEAD OF MY SON!
I WILL WAIT ON YOU HAND AND FOOT UNTIL THE END OF MY DAYS. SPARE THE INNOCENT!
COUNTLESS PALACES, TREASURES, AND SERVANTS — THE WATER SPIRIT HAD EVERYTHING HE WANTED IN HIS UNDERWATER REALM.
HOWEVER...
I SEE YOU ARE A GOOD MAN, MERCHANT. AND YOU KNOW HOW TO BARGAIN. I SHALL SPARE YOUR FAMILY, IF YOU GIVE UP YOUR LIFE RIGHT HERE AND NOW. WHAT DO YOU SAY?
WHAT?
NO!
I AM READY.

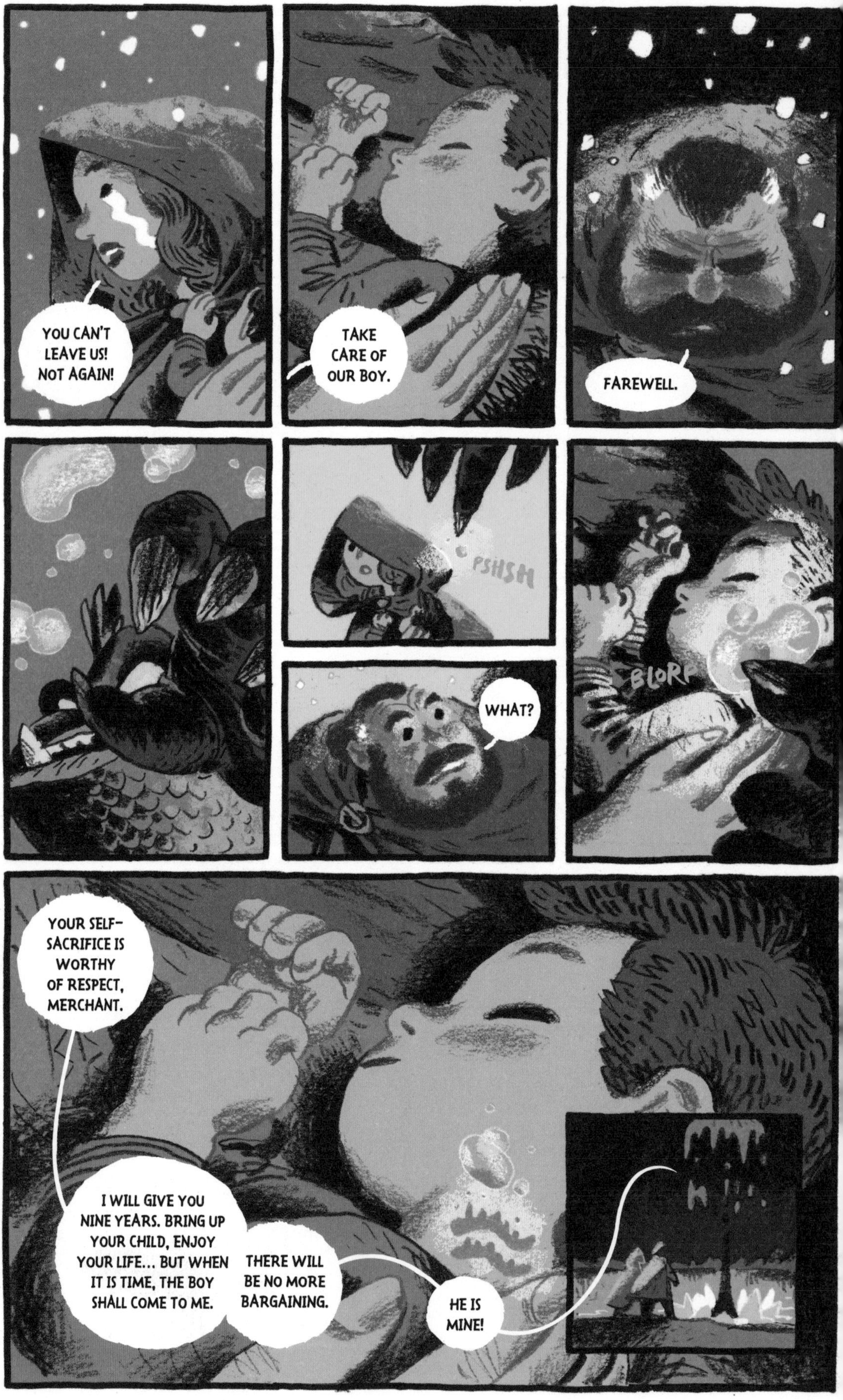
YOU CAN'T LEAVE US! NOT AGAIN!
TAKE CARE OF OUR BOY.
FAREWELL.
PSHSH
WHAT?
BLORP
YOUR SELF-SACRIFICE IS WORTHY OF RESPECT, MERCHANT.
I WILL GIVE YOU NINE YEARS. BRING UP YOUR CHILD, ENJOY YOUR LIFE... BUT WHEN IT IS TIME, THE BOY SHALL COME TO ME.
THERE WILL BE NO MORE BARGAINING.
HE IS MINE!

THE HOUSE SPIRIT

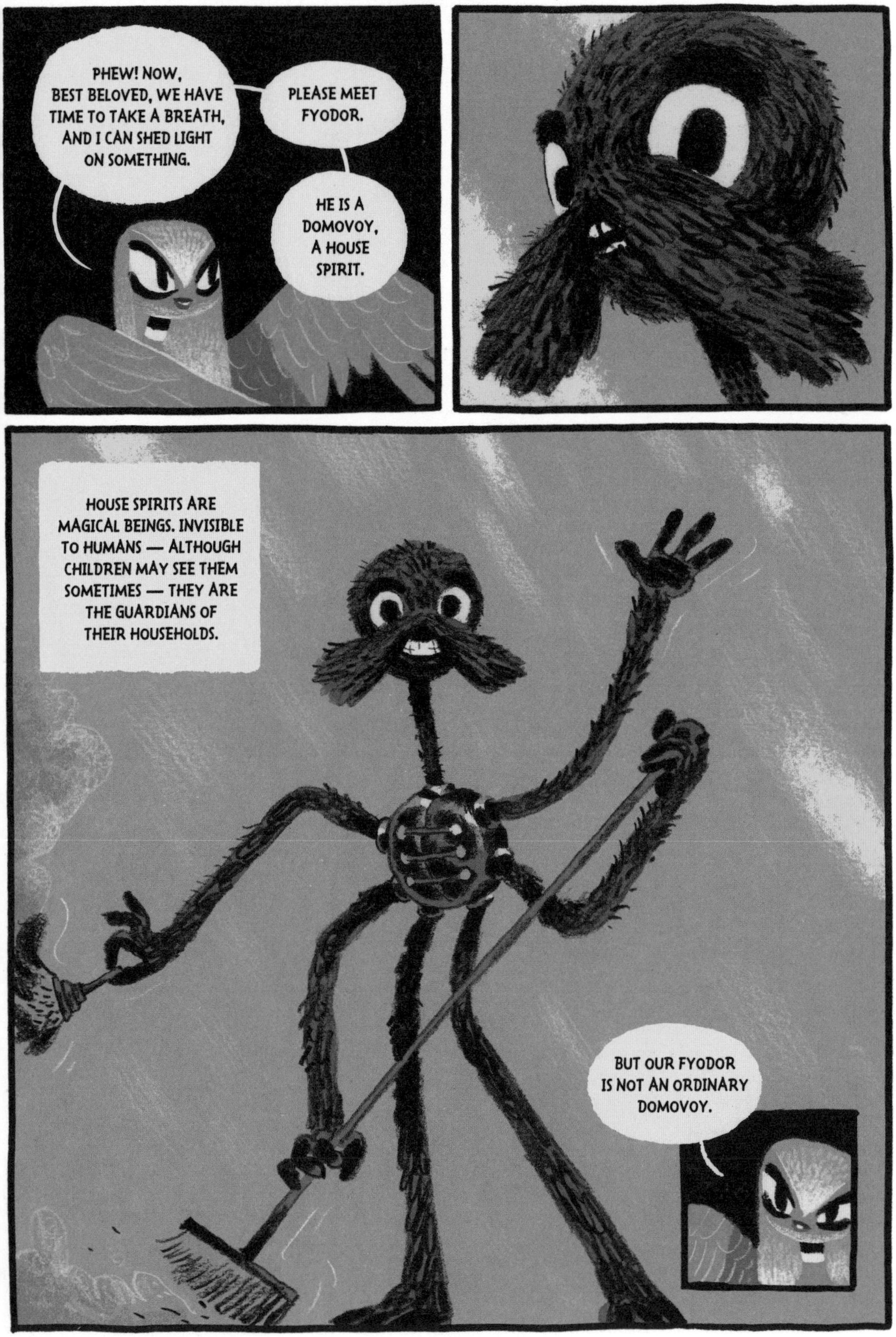

PHEW! NOW, BEST BELOVED, WE HAVE TIME TO TAKE A BREATH, AND I CAN SHED LIGHT ON SOMETHING.
PLEASE MEET FYODOR.
HE IS A DOMOVOY, A HOUSE SPIRIT.
HOUSE SPIRITS ARE MAGICAL BEINGS. INVISIBLE TO HUMANS — ALTHOUGH CHILDREN MAY SEE THEM SOMETIMES — THEY ARE THE GUARDIANS OF THEIR HOUSEHOLDS.
BUT OUR FYODOR IS NOT AN ORDINARY DOMOVOY.

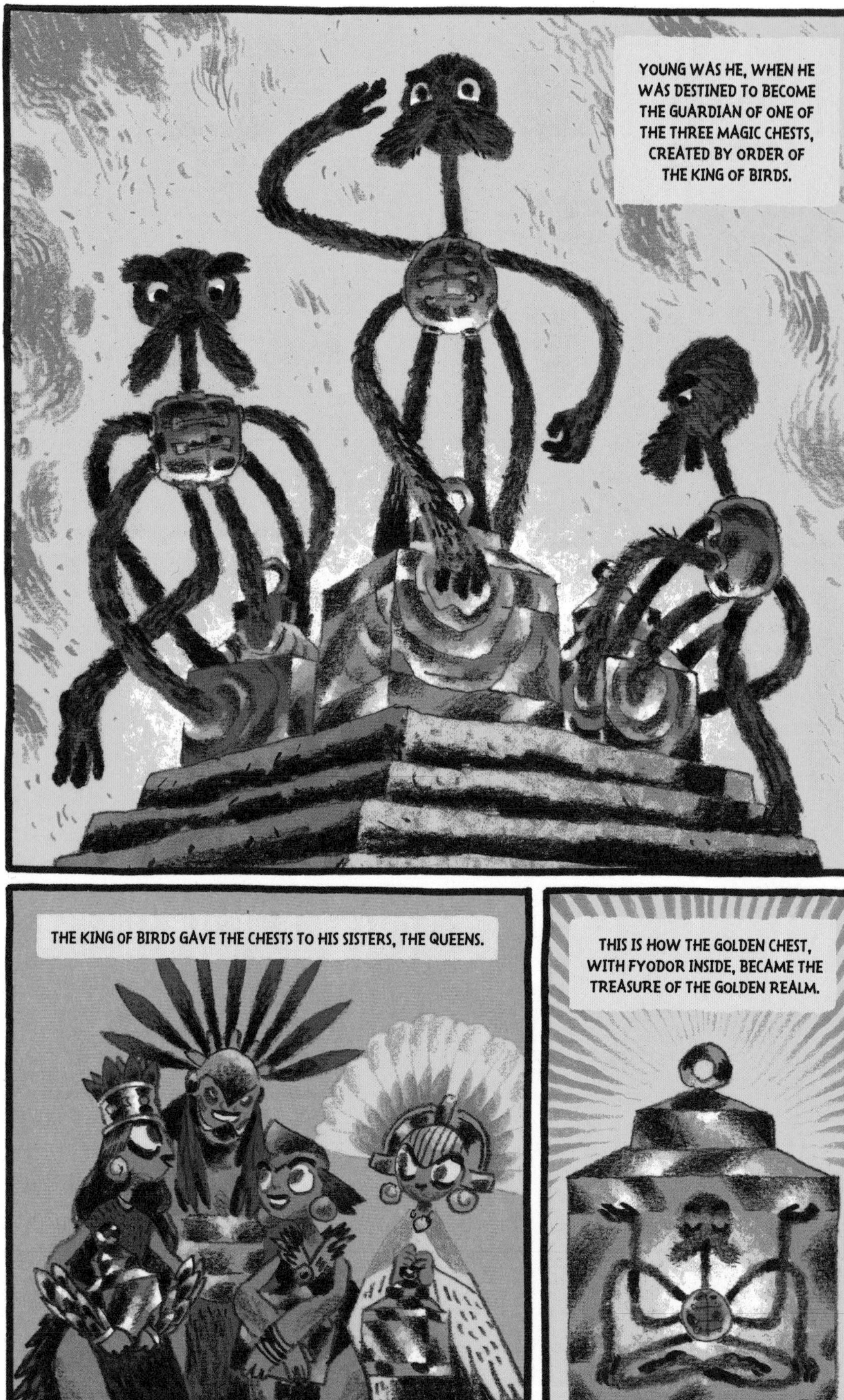
YOUNG WAS HE, WHEN HE WAS DESTINED TO BECOME THE GUARDIAN OF ONE OF THE THREE MAGIC CHESTS, CREATED BY ORDER OF THE KING OF BIRDS.
THE KING OF BIRDS GAVE THE CHESTS TO HIS SISTERS, THE QUEENS.
THIS IS HOW THE GOLDEN CHEST, WITH FYODOR INSIDE, BECAME THE TREASURE OF THE GOLDEN REALM.

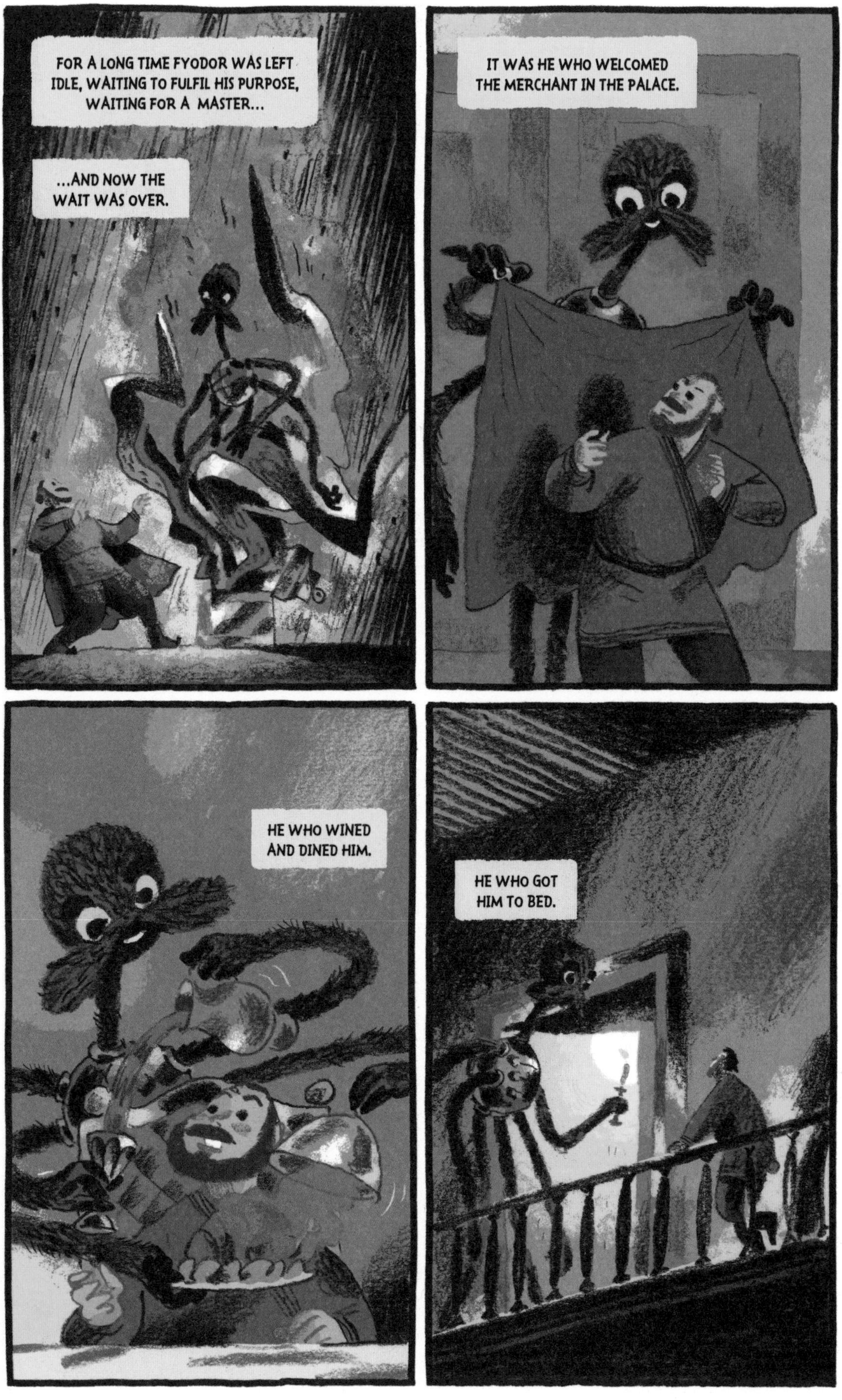

FOR A LONG TIME FYODOR WAS LEFT IDLE, WAITING TO FULFIL HIS PURPOSE, WAITING FOR A MASTER...
...AND NOW THE WAIT WAS OVER.
IT WAS HE WHO WELCOMED THE MERCHANT IN THE PALACE.
HE WHO WINED AND DINED HIM.
HE WHO GOT HIM TO BED.

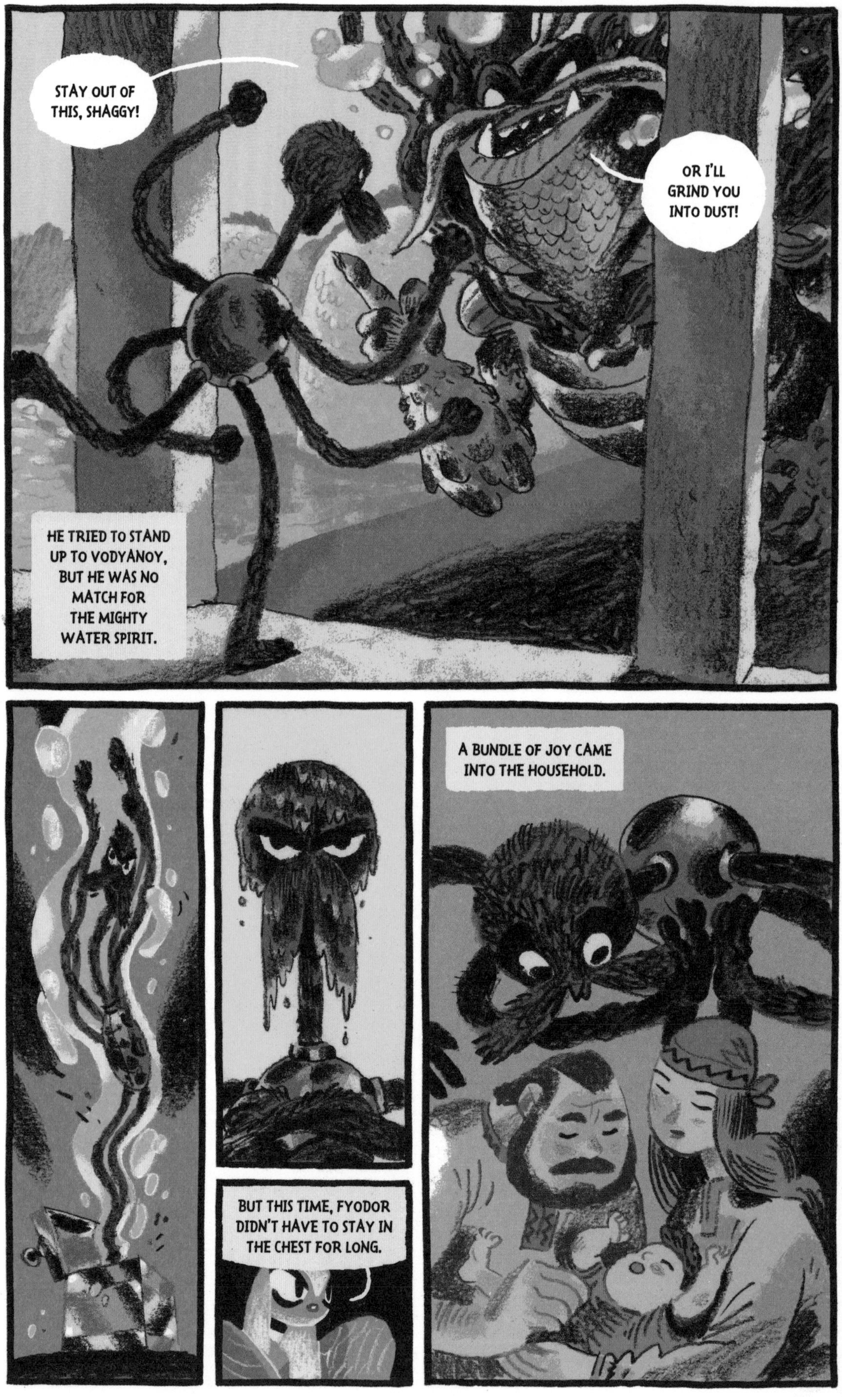
STAY OUT OF THIS, SHAGGY!
OR I'LL GRIND YOU INTO DUST!
HE TRIED TO STAND UP TO VODYANOY, BUT HE WAS NO MATCH FOR THE MIGHTY WATER SPIRIT.
BUT THIS TIME, FYODOR DIDN'T HAVE TO STAY IN THE CHEST FOR LONG.
A BUNDLE OF JOY CAME INTO THE HOUSEHOLD.

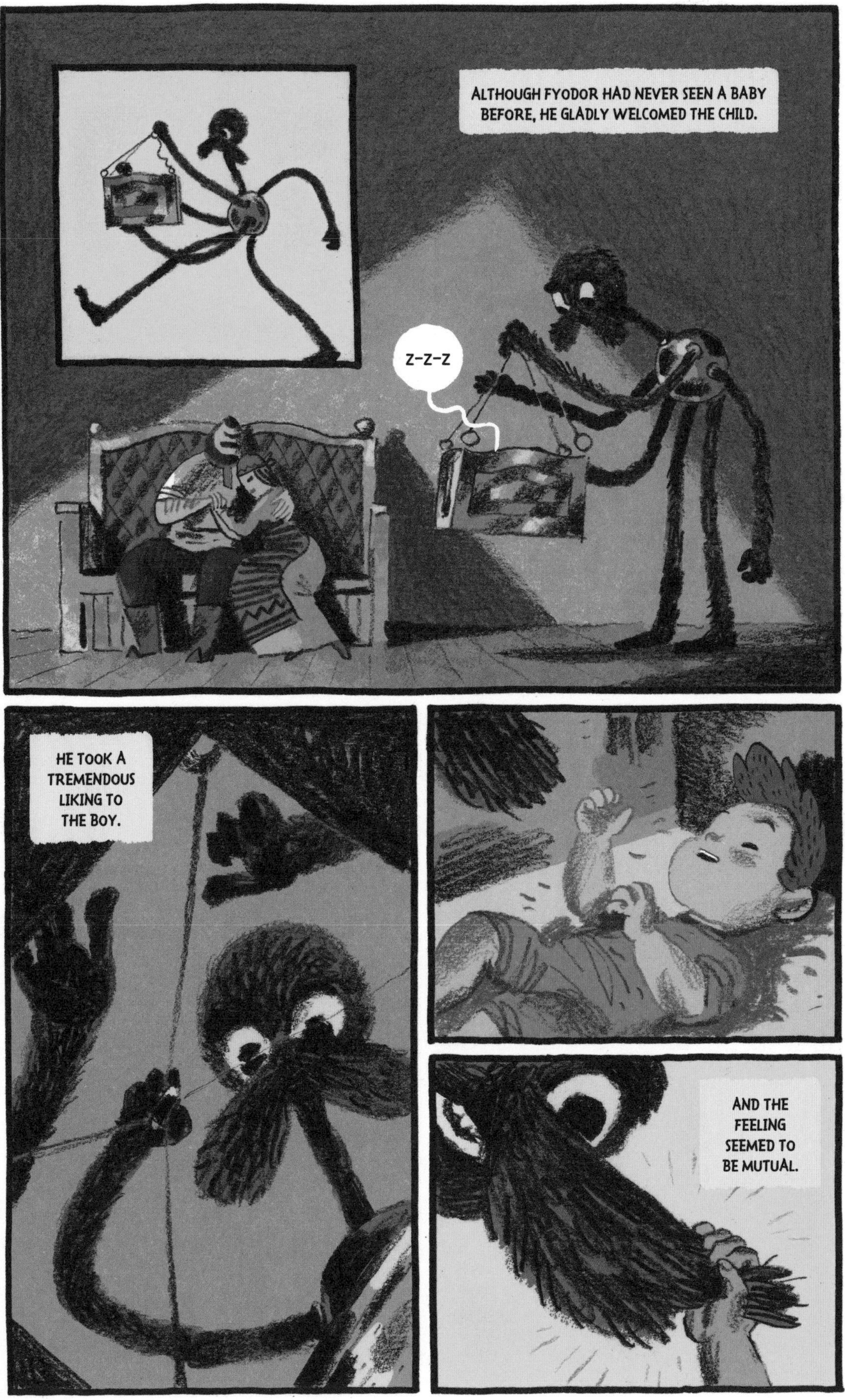
ALTHOUGH FYODOR HAD NEVER SEEN A BABY BEFORE, HE GLADLY WELCOMED THE CHILD.
Z-Z-Z
HE TOOK A TREMENDOUS LIKING TO THE BOY.
AND THE FEELING SEEMED TO BE MUTUAL.

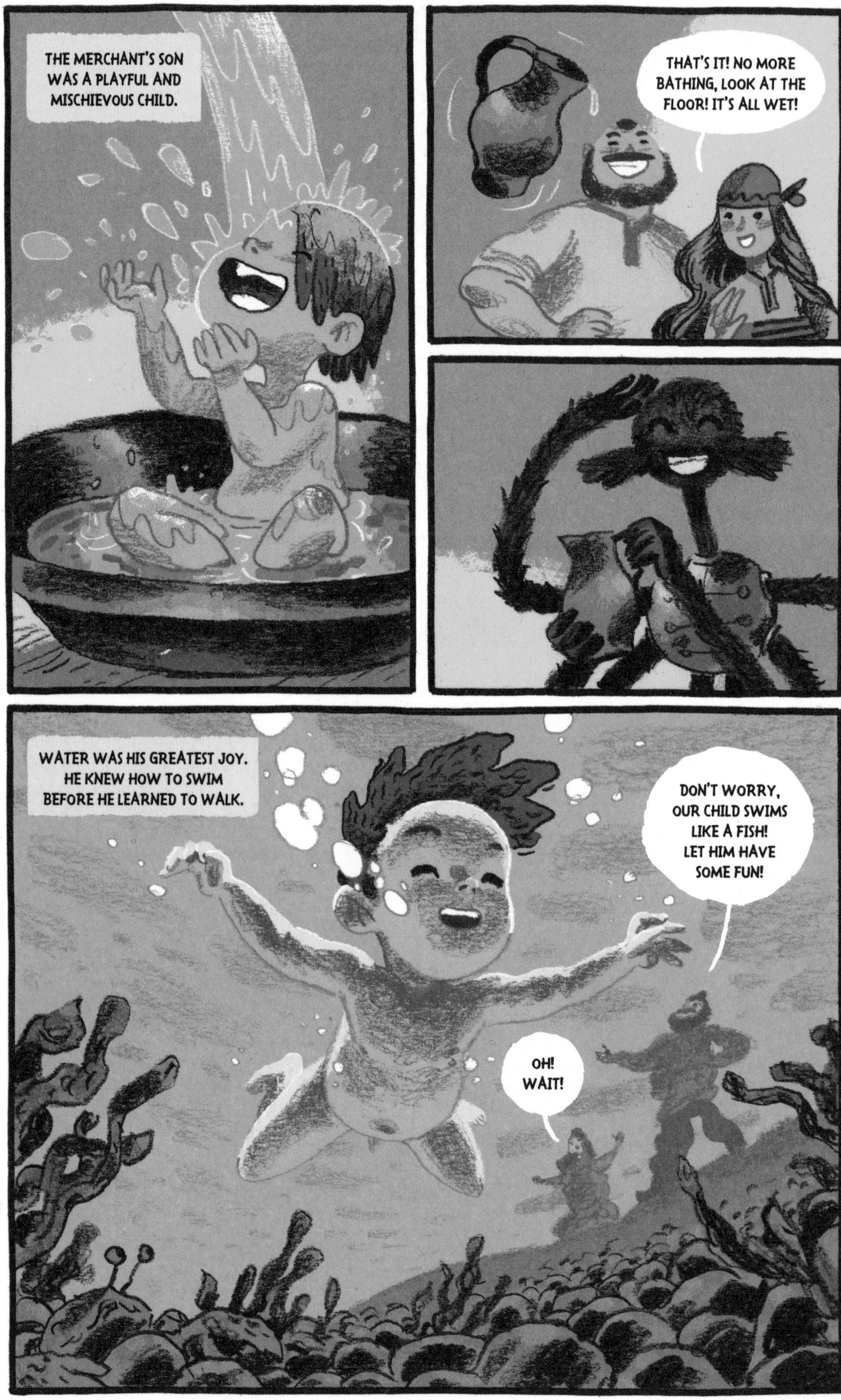
THE MERCHANT'S SON WAS A PLAYFUL AND MISCHIEVOUS CHILD.
THAT'S IT! NO MORE BATHING, LOOK AT THE FLOOR! IT'S ALL WET!
WATER WAS HIS GREATEST JOY. HE KNEW HOW TO SWIM BEFORE HE LEARNED TO WALK.
DON'T WORRY, OUR CHILD SWIMS LIKE A FISH! LET HIM HAVE SOME FUN!
OH! WAIT!

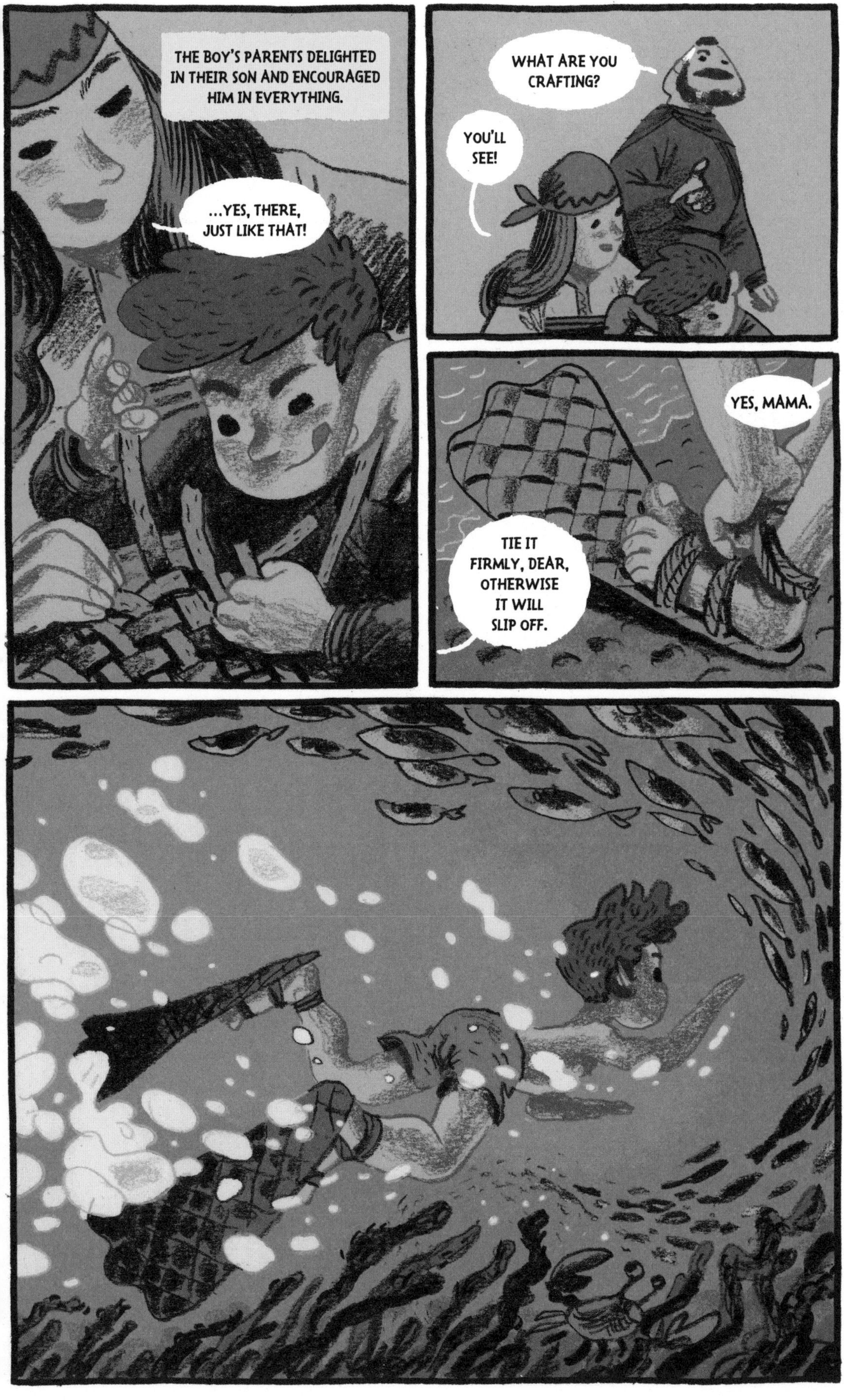
THE BOY'S PARENTS DELIGHTED IN THEIR SON AND ENCOURAGED HIM IN EVERYTHING.
...YES, THERE, JUST LIKE THAT!
WHAT ARE YOU CRAFTING?
YOU'LL SEE!
YES, MAMA.
TIE IT FIRMLY, DEAR, OTHERWISE IT WILL SLIP OFF.

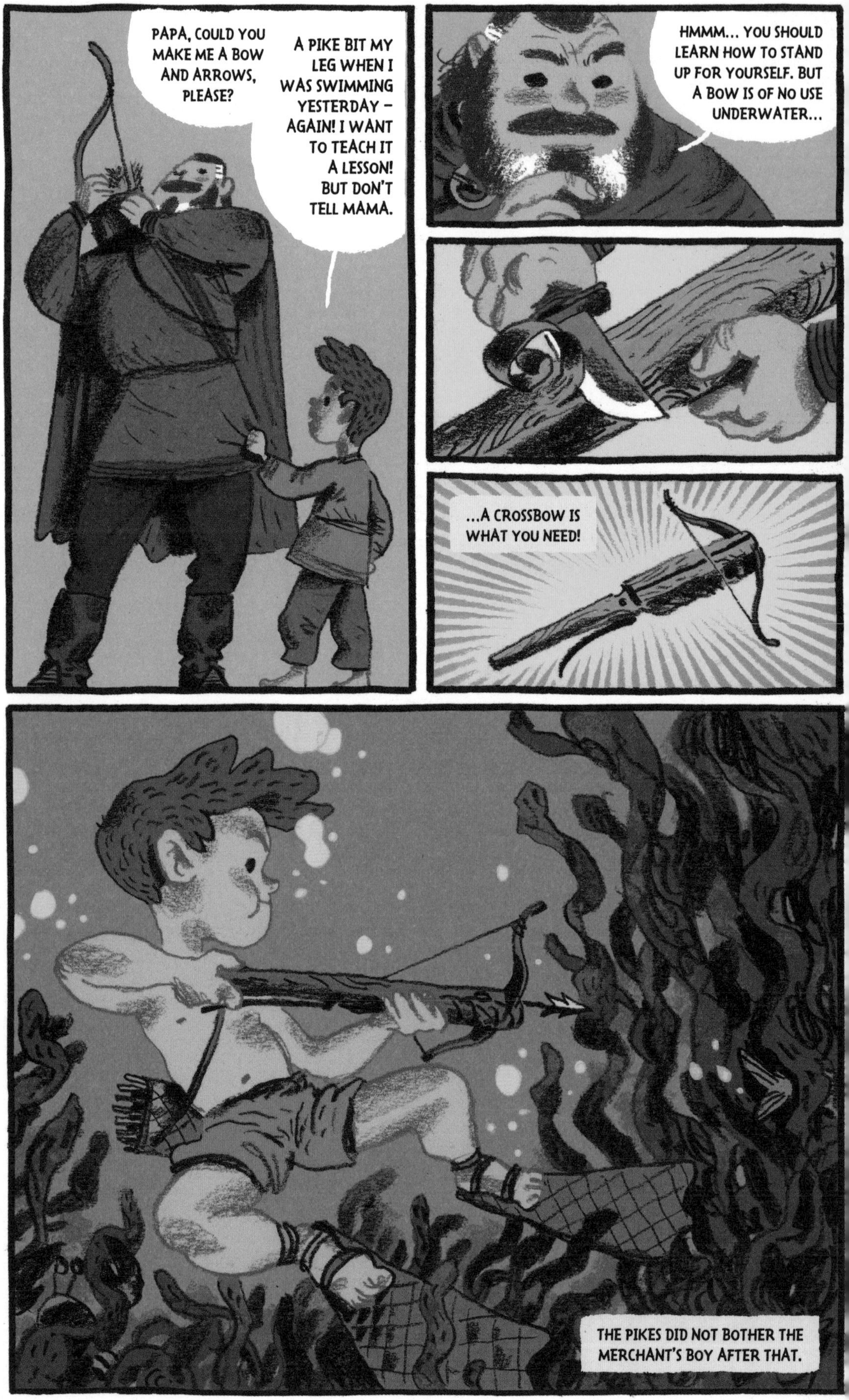
PAPA, COULD YOU MAKE ME A BOW AND ARROWS, PLEASE?
A PIKE BIT MY LEG WHEN I WAS SWIMMING YESTERDAY – AGAIN! I WANT TO TEACH IT A LESSON! BUT DON'T TELL MAMA.
HMMM... YOU SHOULD LEARN HOW TO STAND UP FOR YOURSELF. BUT A BOW IS OF NO USE UNDERWATER...
...A CROSSBOW IS WHAT YOU NEED!
THE PIKES DID NOT BOTHER THE MERCHANT'S BOY AFTER THAT.

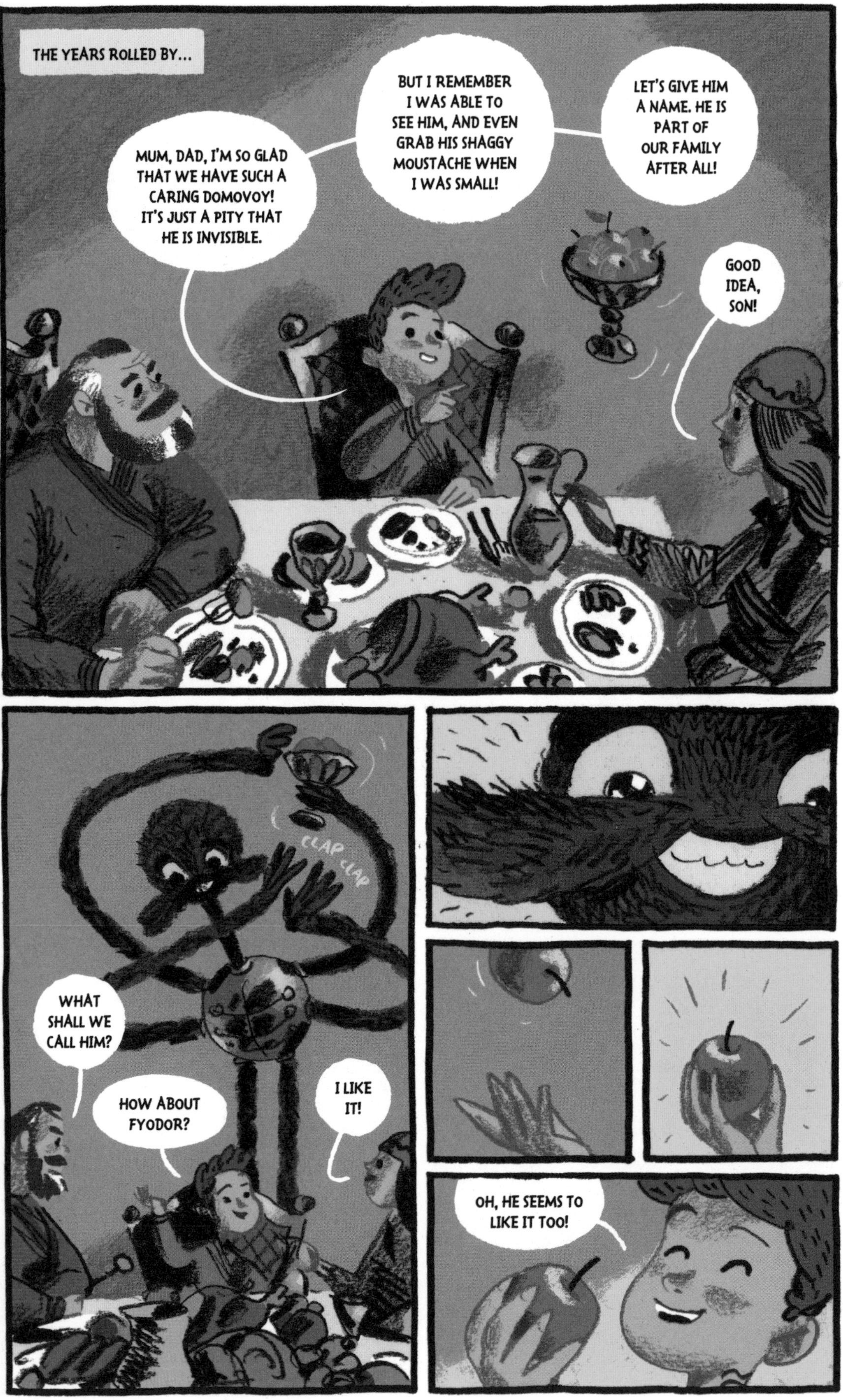
THE YEARS ROLLED BY...
MUM, DAD, I'M SO GLAD THAT WE HAVE SUCH A CARING DOMOVOY! IT'S JUST A PITY THAT HE IS INVISIBLE.
BUT I REMEMBER I WAS ABLE TO SEE HIM, AND EVEN GRAB HIS SHAGGY MOUSTACHE WHEN I WAS SMALL!
LET'S GIVE HIM A NAME. HE IS PART OF OUR FAMILY AFTER ALL!
GOOD IDEA, SON!
CLAP CLAP
WHAT SHALL WE CALL HIM?
HOW ABOUT FYODOR?
I LIKE IT!
OH, HE SEEMS TO LIKE IT TOO!

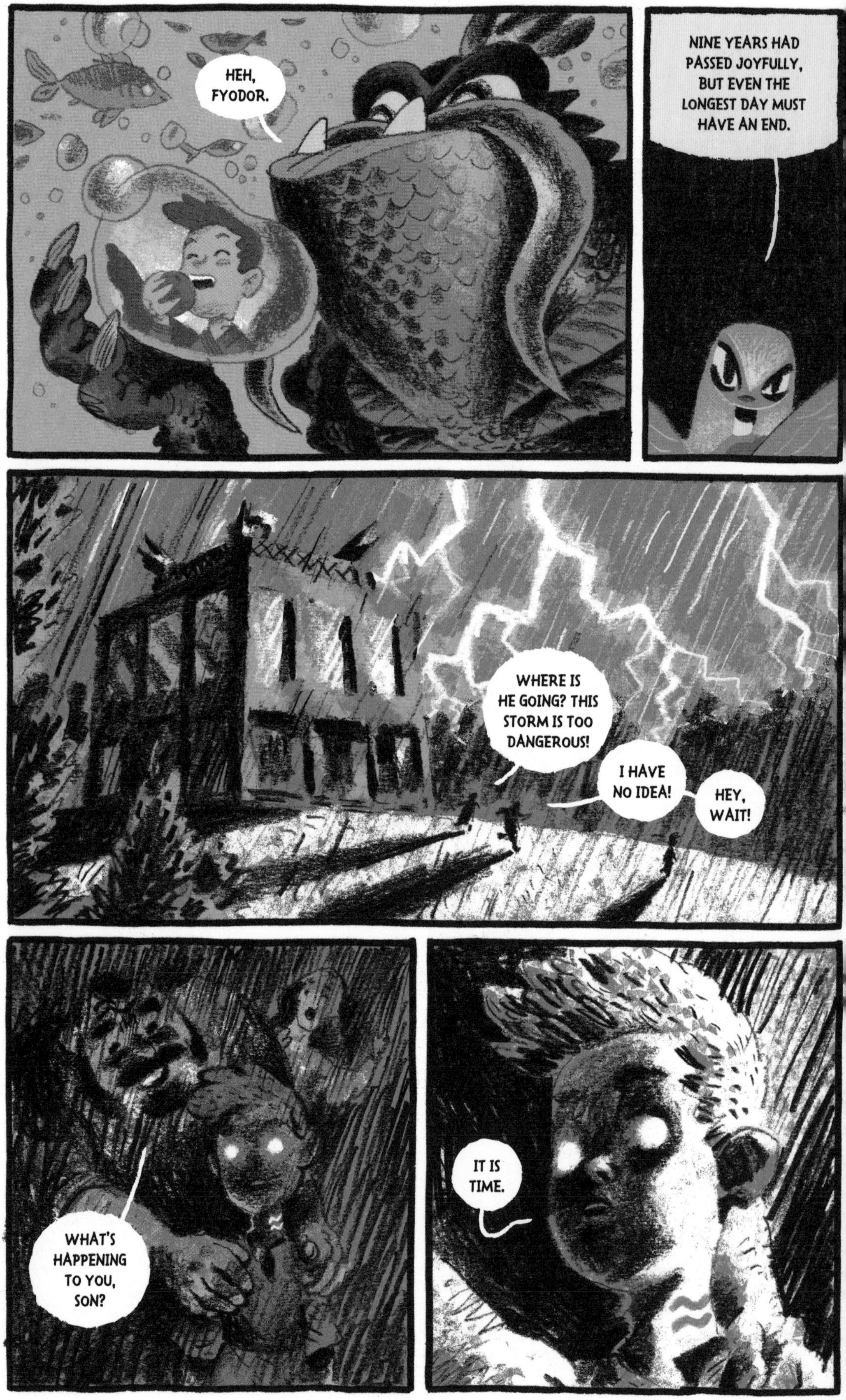
HEH, FYODOR.
NINE YEARS HAD PASSED JOYFULLY, BUT EVEN THE LONGEST DAY MUST HAVE AN END.
WHERE IS HE GOING? THIS STORM IS TOO DANGEROUS!
I HAVE NO IDEA!
HEY, WAIT!
WHAT'S HAPPENING TO YOU, SON?
IT IS TIME.

THE SACRED LAKE

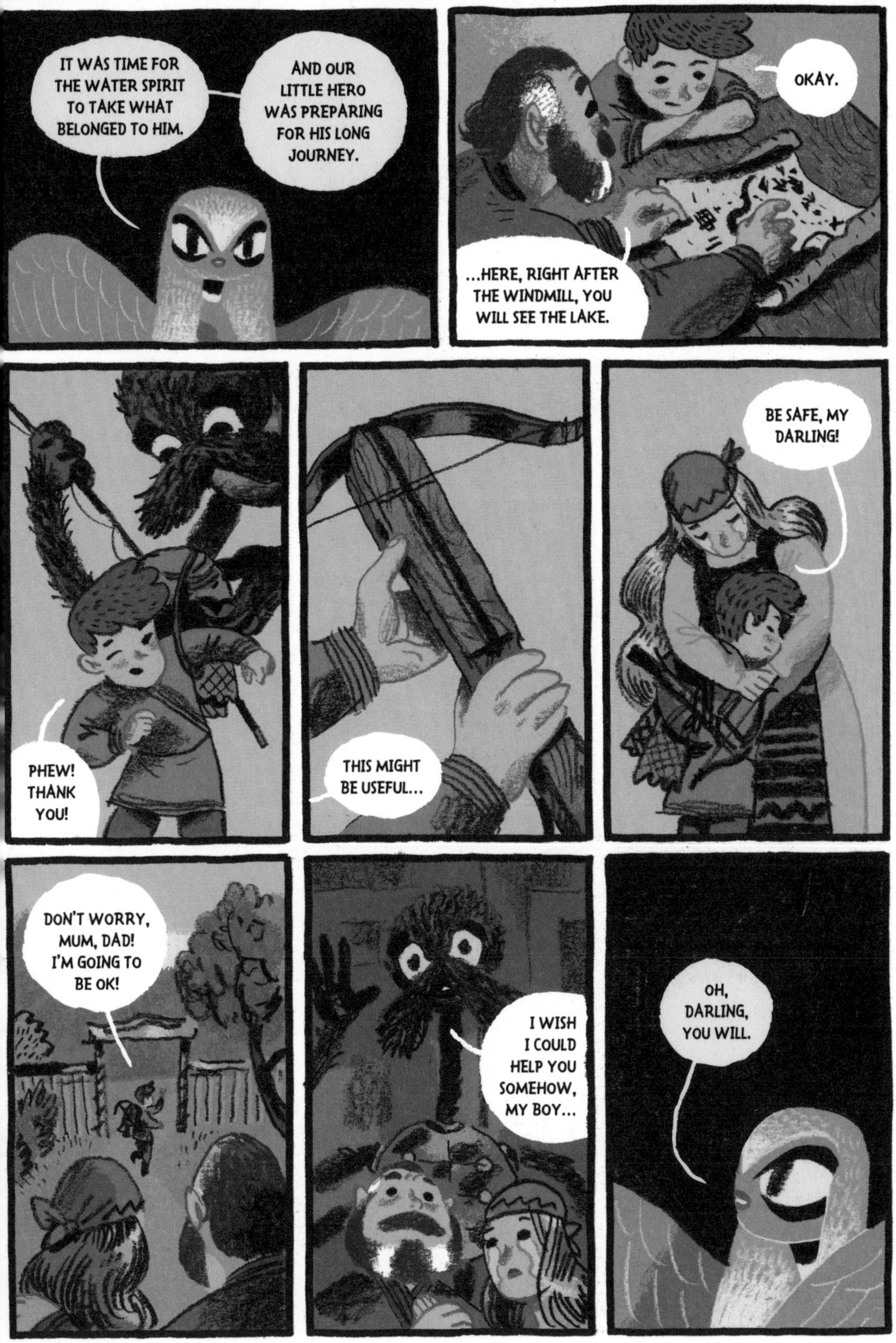

IT WAS TIME FOR THE WATER SPIRIT TO TAKE WHAT BELONGED TO HIM.
AND OUR LITTLE HERO WAS PREPARING FOR HIS LONG JOURNEY.
OKAY.
...HERE, RIGHT AFTER THE WINDMILL, YOU WILL SEE THE LAKE.
PHEW! THANK YOU!
THIS MIGHT BE USEFUL...
BE SAFE, MY DARLING!
DON'T WORRY, MUM, DAD! I'M GOING TO BE OK!
I WISH I COULD HELP YOU SOMEHOW, MY BOY...
OH, DARLING, YOU WILL.

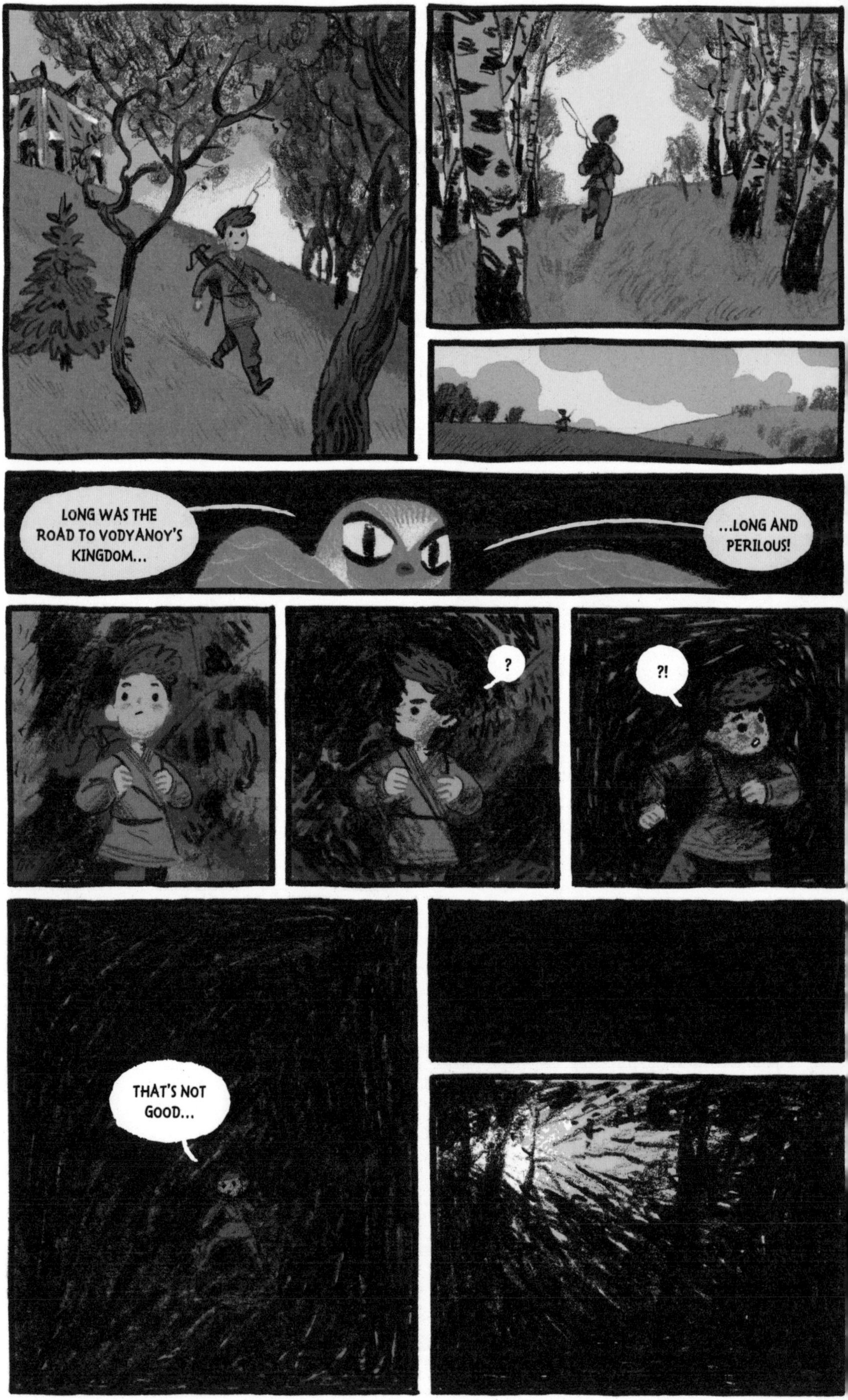

LONG WAS THE ROAD TO VODYANOY'S KINGDOM...
...LONG AND PERILOUS!
?
?!
THAT'S NOT GOOD...

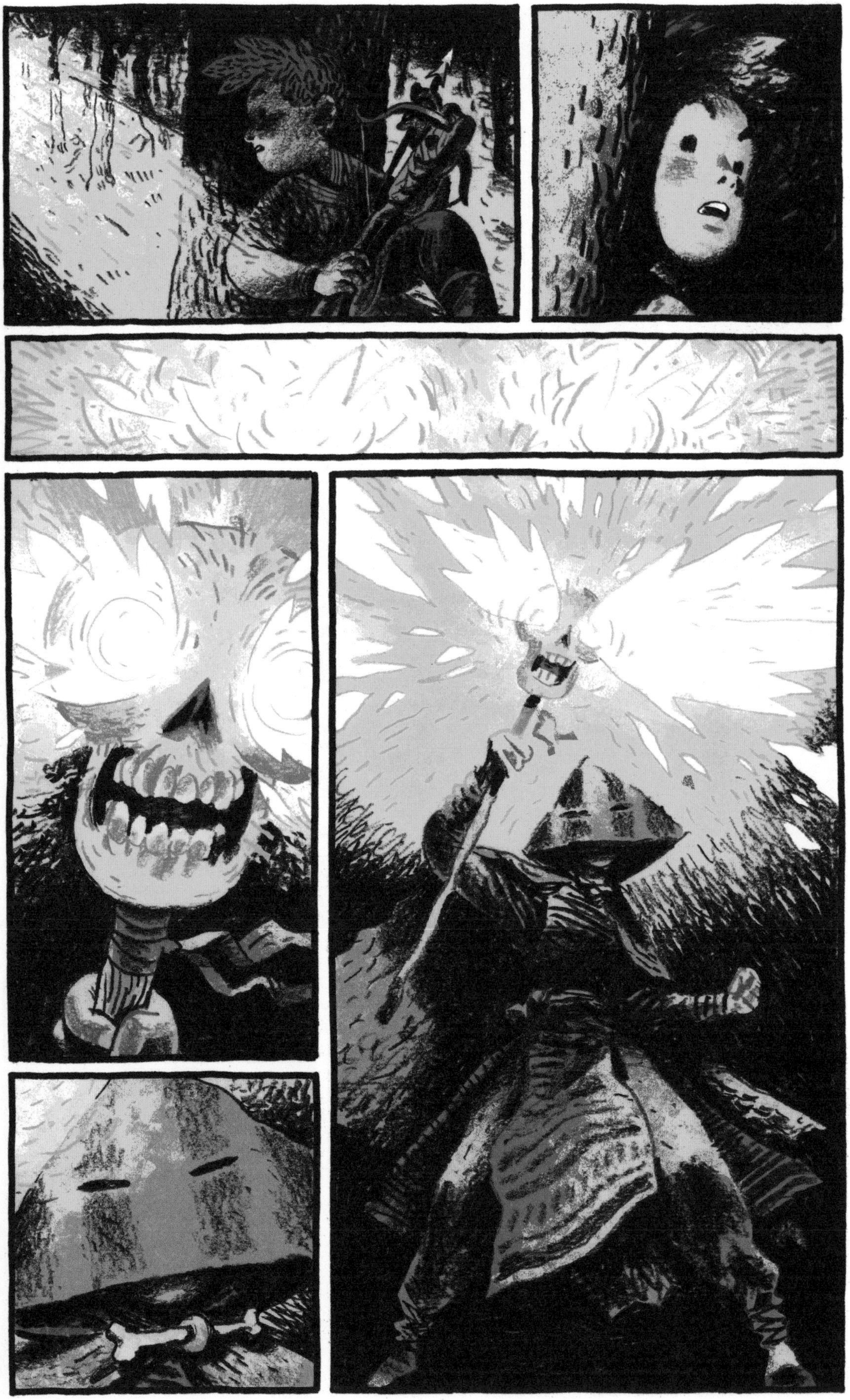

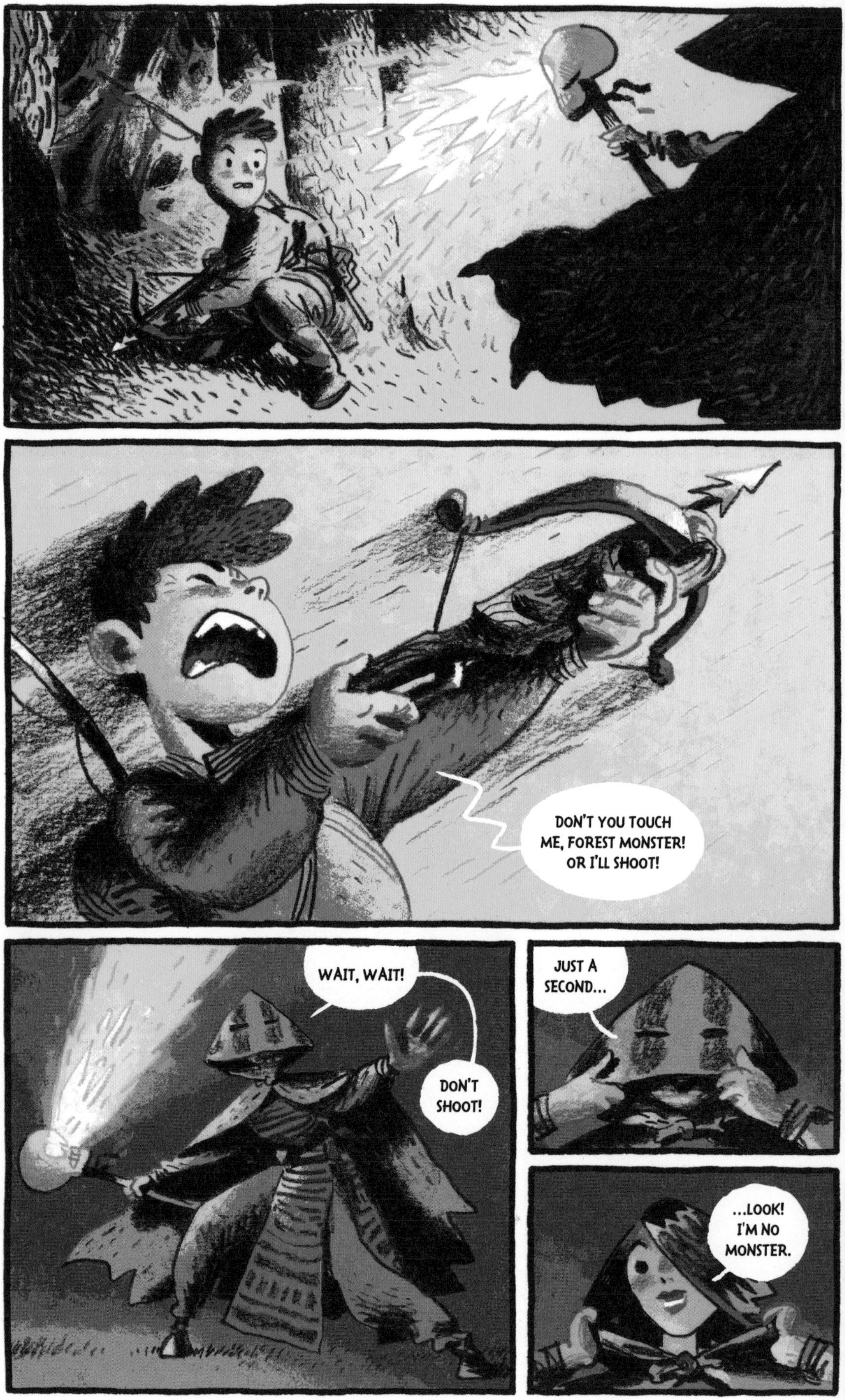

DON'T YOU TOUCH ME, FOREST MONSTER! OR I'LL SHOOT!
WAIT, WAIT!
DON'T SHOOT!
JUST A SECOND...
...LOOK! I'M NO MONSTER.

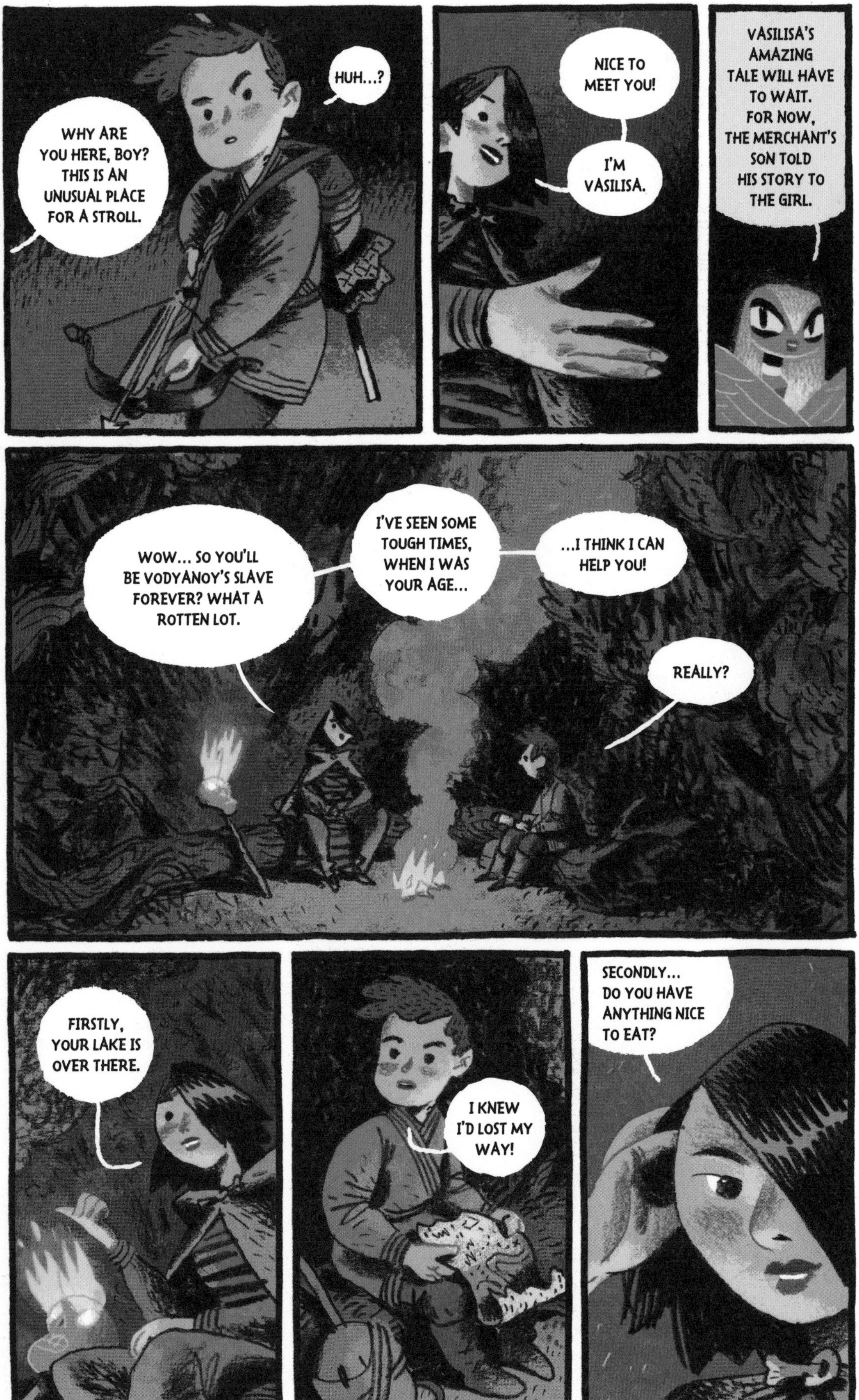

WHY ARE YOU HERE, BOY? THIS IS AN UNUSUAL PLACE FOR A STROLL.
HUH...?
NICE TO MEET YOU!
I'M VASILISA.
VASILISA'S AMAZING TALE WILL HAVE TO WAIT. FOR NOW, THE MERCHANT'S SON TOLD HIS STORY TO THE GIRL.
WOW... SO YOU'LL BE VODYANOY'S SLAVE FOREVER? WHAT A ROTTEN LOT.
I'VE SEEN SOME TOUGH TIMES, WHEN I WAS YOUR AGE...
...I THINK I CAN HELP YOU!
REALLY?
FIRSTLY, YOUR LAKE IS OVER THERE.
I KNEW I'D LOST MY WAY!
SECONDLY... DO YOU HAVE ANYTHING NICE TO EAT?

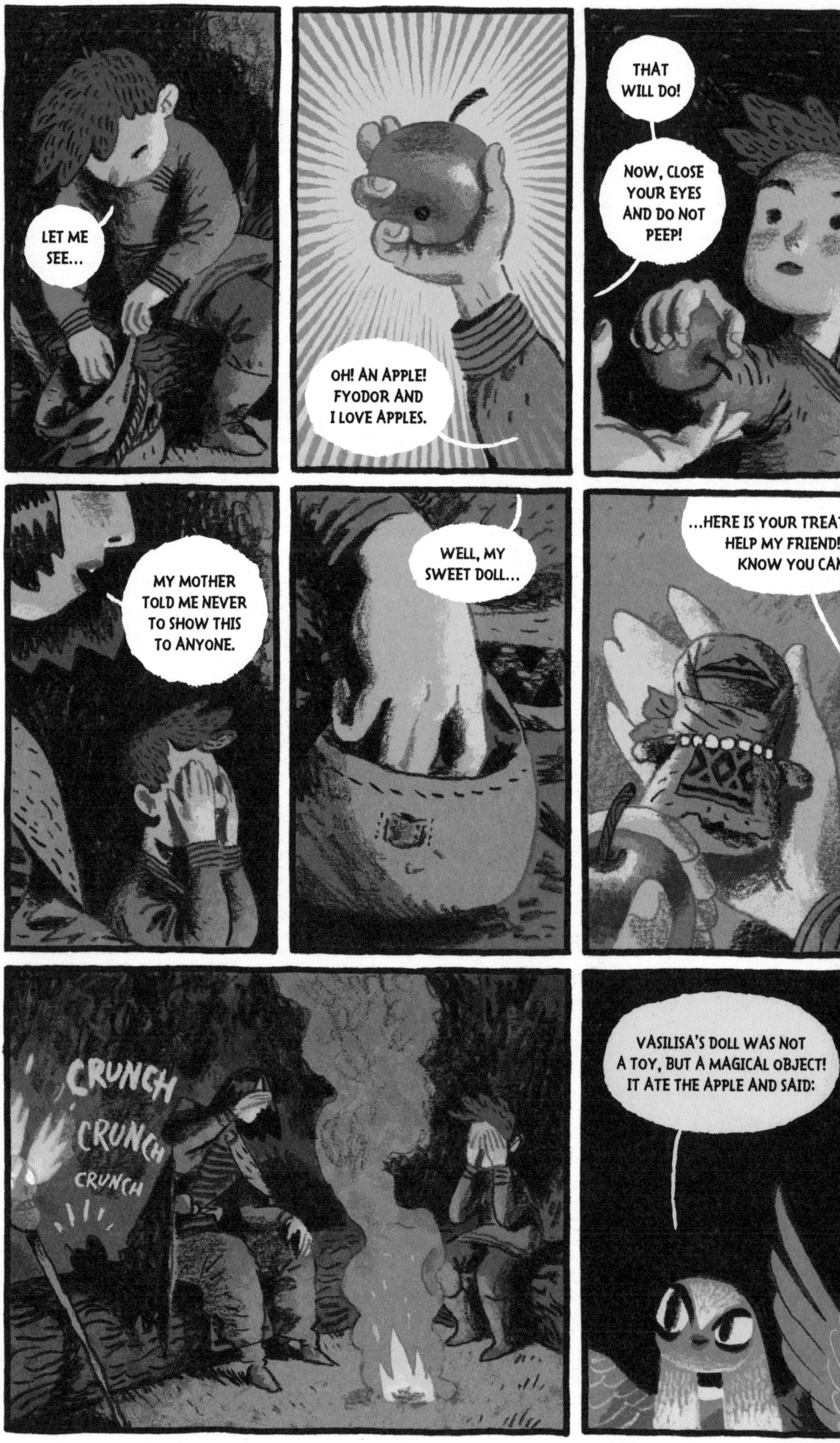
LET ME SEE...
OH! AN APPLE! FYODOR AND I LOVE APPLES.
THAT WILL DO!
NOW, CLOSE YOUR EYES AND DO NOT PEEP!
MY MOTHER TOLD ME NEVER TO SHOW THIS TO ANYONE.
WELL, MY SWEET DOLL...
...HERE IS YOUR TREAT. HELP MY FRIEND! I KNOW YOU CAN.
CRUNCH
CRUNCH
CRUNCH
VASILISA'S DOLL WAS NOT A TOY, BUT A MAGICAL OBJECT! IT ATE THE APPLE AND SAID:

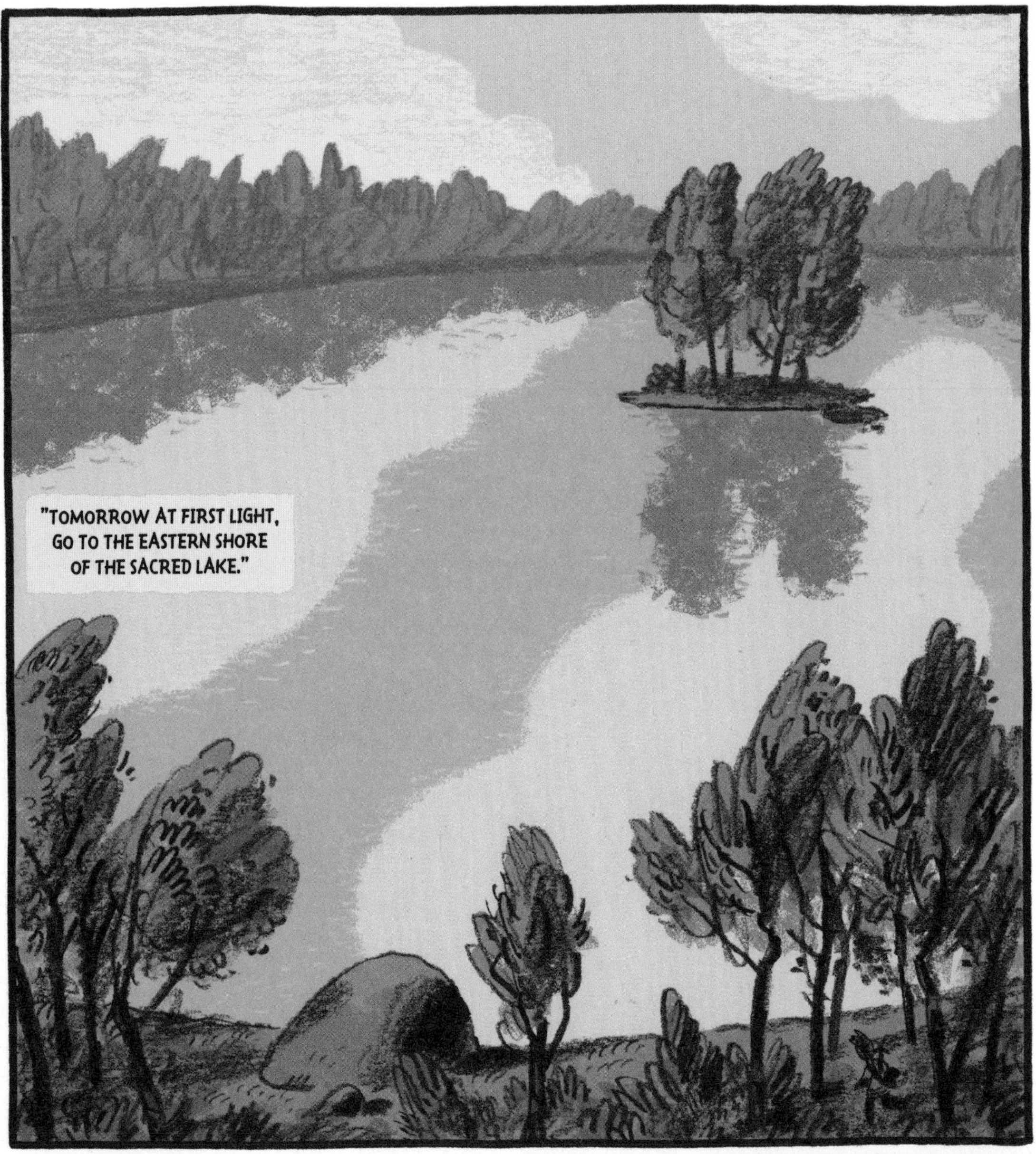
"TOMORROW AT FIRST LIGHT, GO TO THE EASTERN SHORE OF THE SACRED LAKE."

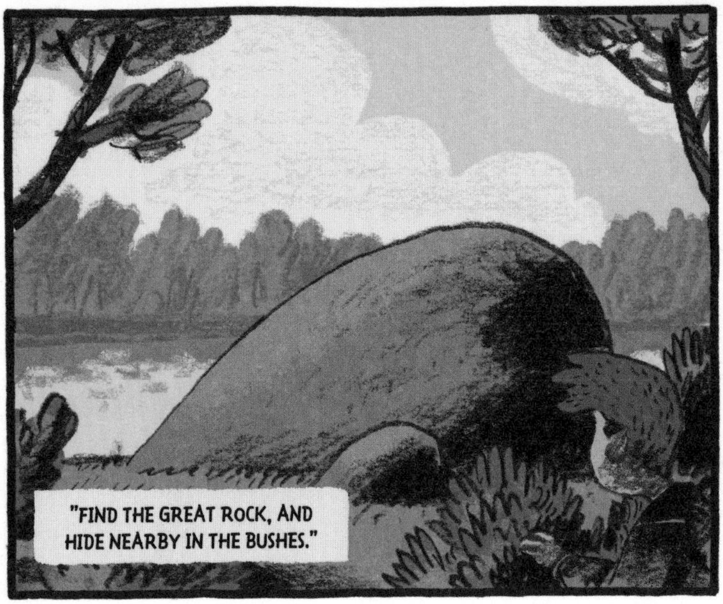
"FIND THE GREAT ROCK, AND HIDE NEARBY IN THE BUSHES."

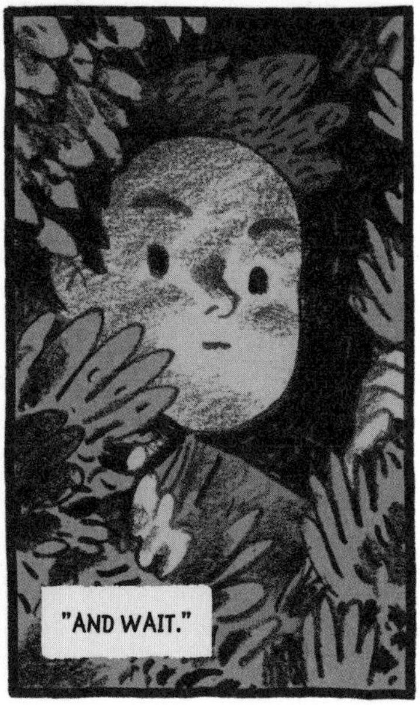
"AND WAIT."

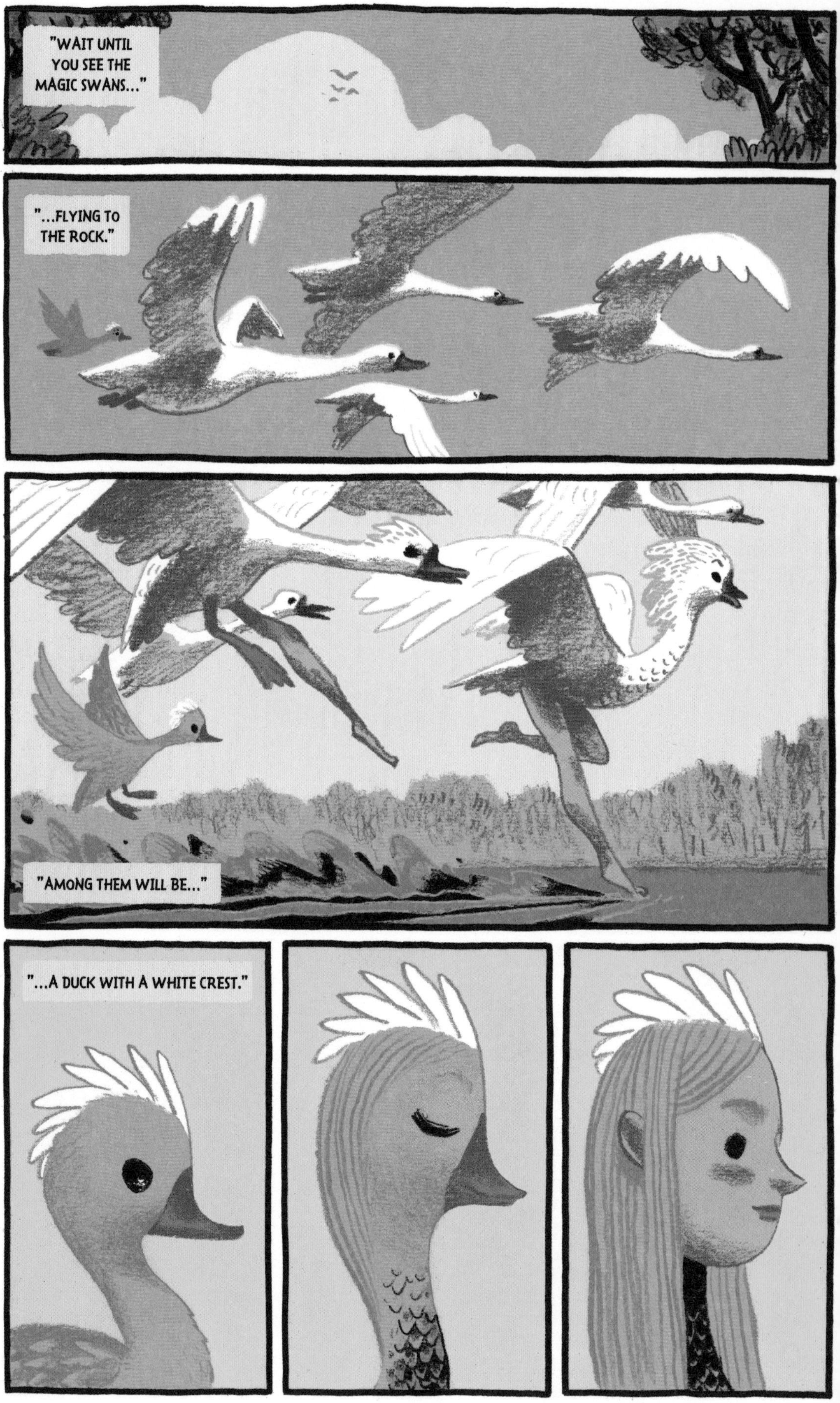
"WAIT UNTIL YOU SEE THE MAGIC SWANS..."
"...FLYING TO THE ROCK."
"AMONG THEM WILL BE..."
"...A DUCK WITH A WHITE CREST."

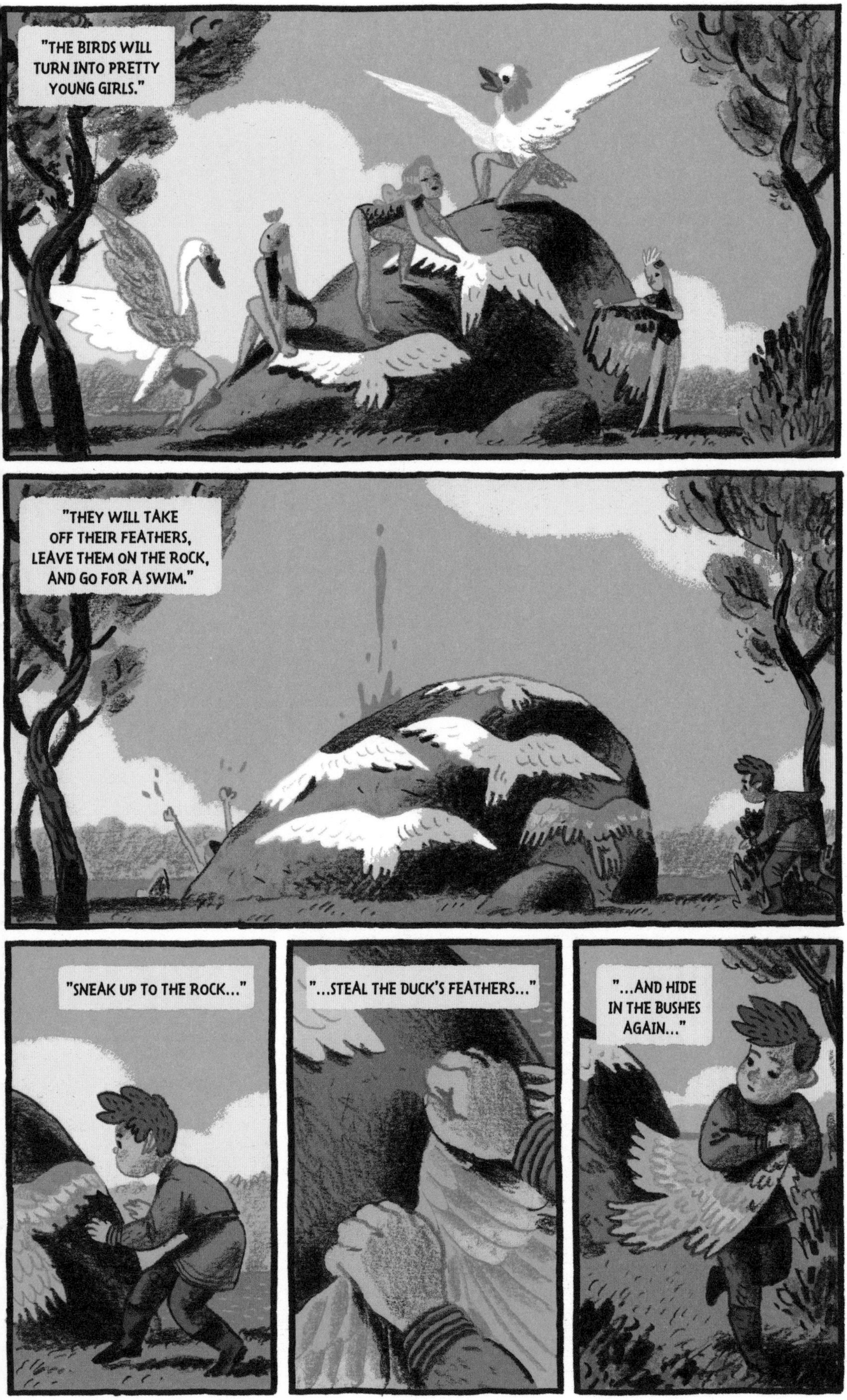
"THE BIRDS WILL TURN INTO PRETTY YOUNG GIRLS."
"THEY WILL TAKE OFF THEIR FEATHERS, LEAVE THEM ON THE ROCK, AND GO FOR A SWIM."
"SNEAK UP TO THE ROCK..."
"...STEAL THE DUCK'S FEATHERS..."
"...AND HIDE IN THE BUSHES AGAIN..."

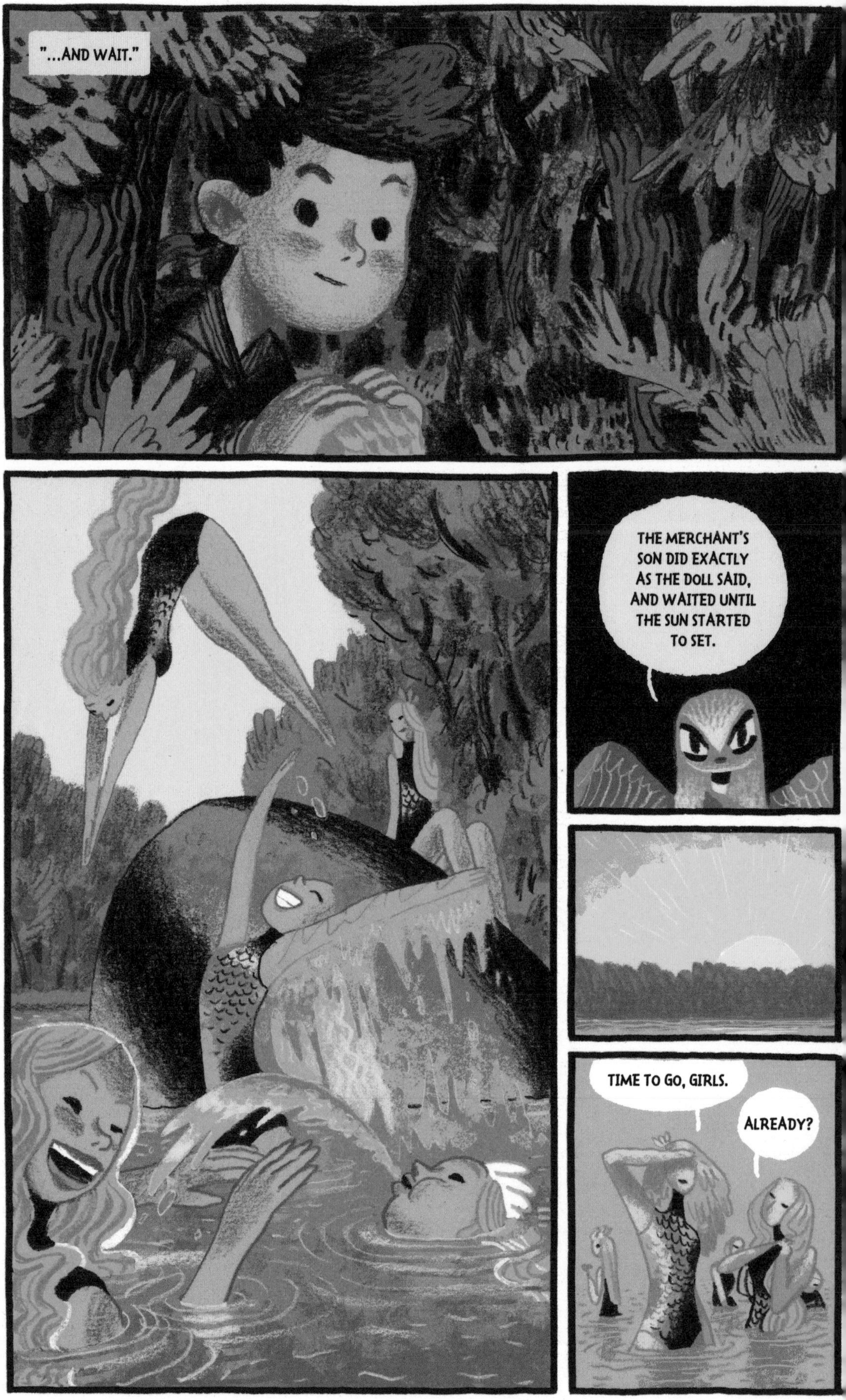
"...AND WAIT."
THE MERCHANT'S SON DID EXACTLY AS THE DOLL SAID, AND WAITED UNTIL THE SUN STARTED TO SET.
TIME TO GO, GIRLS.
ALREADY?

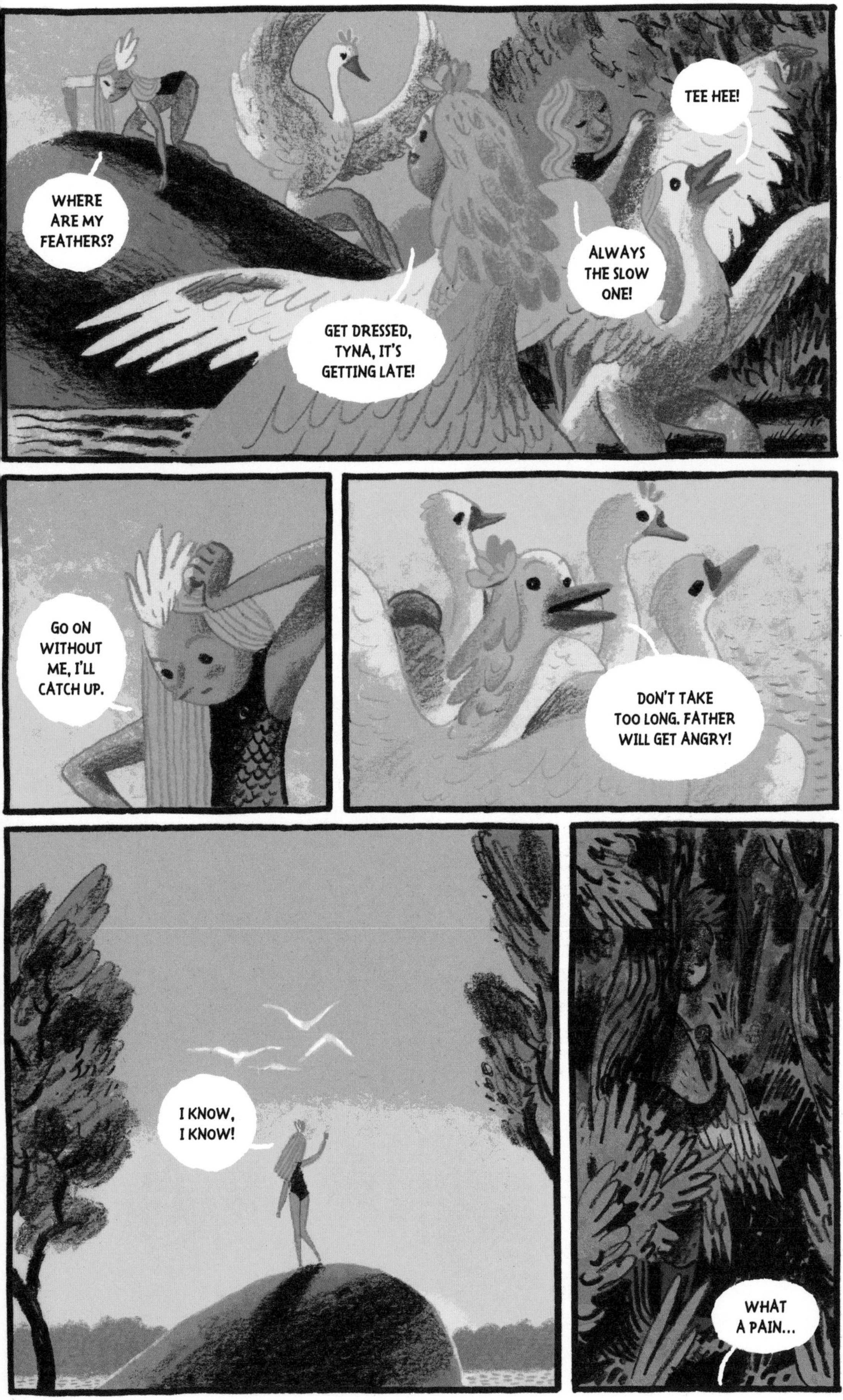
WHERE ARE MY FEATHERS?
GET DRESSED, TYNA, IT'S GETTING LATE!
ALWAYS THE SLOW ONE!
TEE HEE!
GO ON WITHOUT ME, I'LL CATCH UP.
DON'T TAKE TOO LONG. FATHER WILL GET ANGRY!
I KNOW, I KNOW!
WHAT A PAIN...

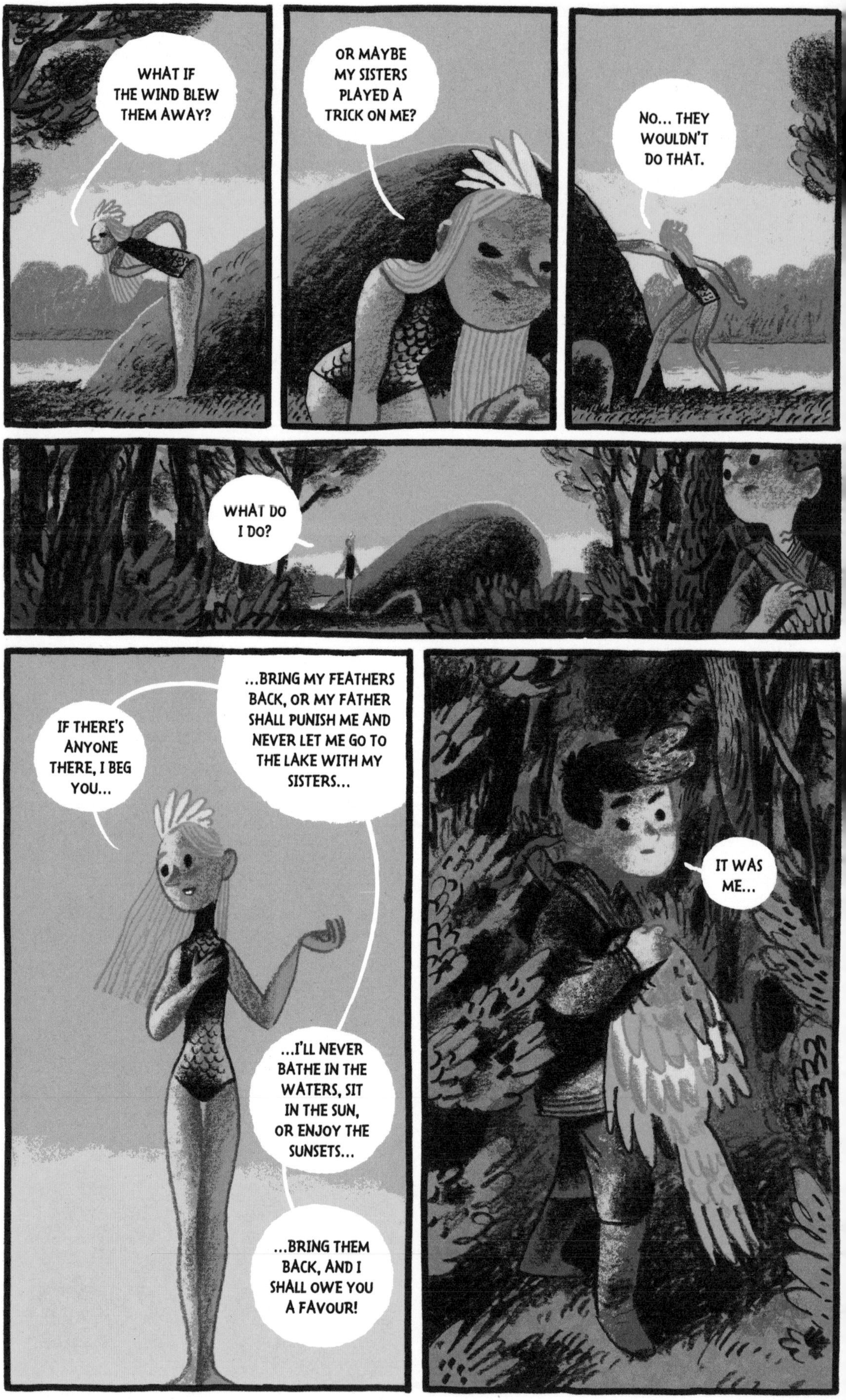
WHAT IF THE WIND BLEW THEM AWAY?
OR MAYBE MY SISTERS PLAYED A TRICK ON ME?
NO... THEY WOULDN'T DO THAT.
WHAT DO I DO?
IF THERE'S ANYONE THERE, I BEG YOU...
...BRING MY FEATHERS BACK, OR MY FATHER SHALL PUNISH ME AND NEVER LET ME GO TO THE LAKE WITH MY SISTERS...
...I'LL NEVER BATHE IN THE WATERS, SIT IN THE SUN, OR ENJOY THE SUNSETS...
...BRING THEM BACK, AND I SHALL OWE YOU A FAVOUR!
IT WAS ME...

...I DIDN'T MEAN TO...

...A DOLL MADE ME DO IT...!

AND THE MERCHANT'S SON TOLD EVERYTHING TO TYNA; HE TOLD HER ABOUT HIS FATHER AND THE PALACE-IN-A-CHEST, ABOUT THE EVIL VODYANOY AND THE GOOD DOMOVOY, AND ABOUT VASILISA AND THE DOLL.

YOU? BUT HOW?

IT IS NOT FAIR THAT YOU'RE PAYING FOR SOMEONE ELSE'S MISTAKES!

I CANNOT ALLOW THAT!

FOR A START, TAKE THIS...

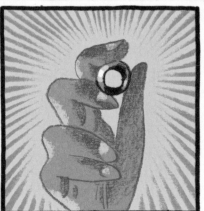

WITH THIS RING, YOU WILL BE ABLE TO BREATHE UNDERWATER AND RESIST VODYANOY'S MAGIC SPELLS.

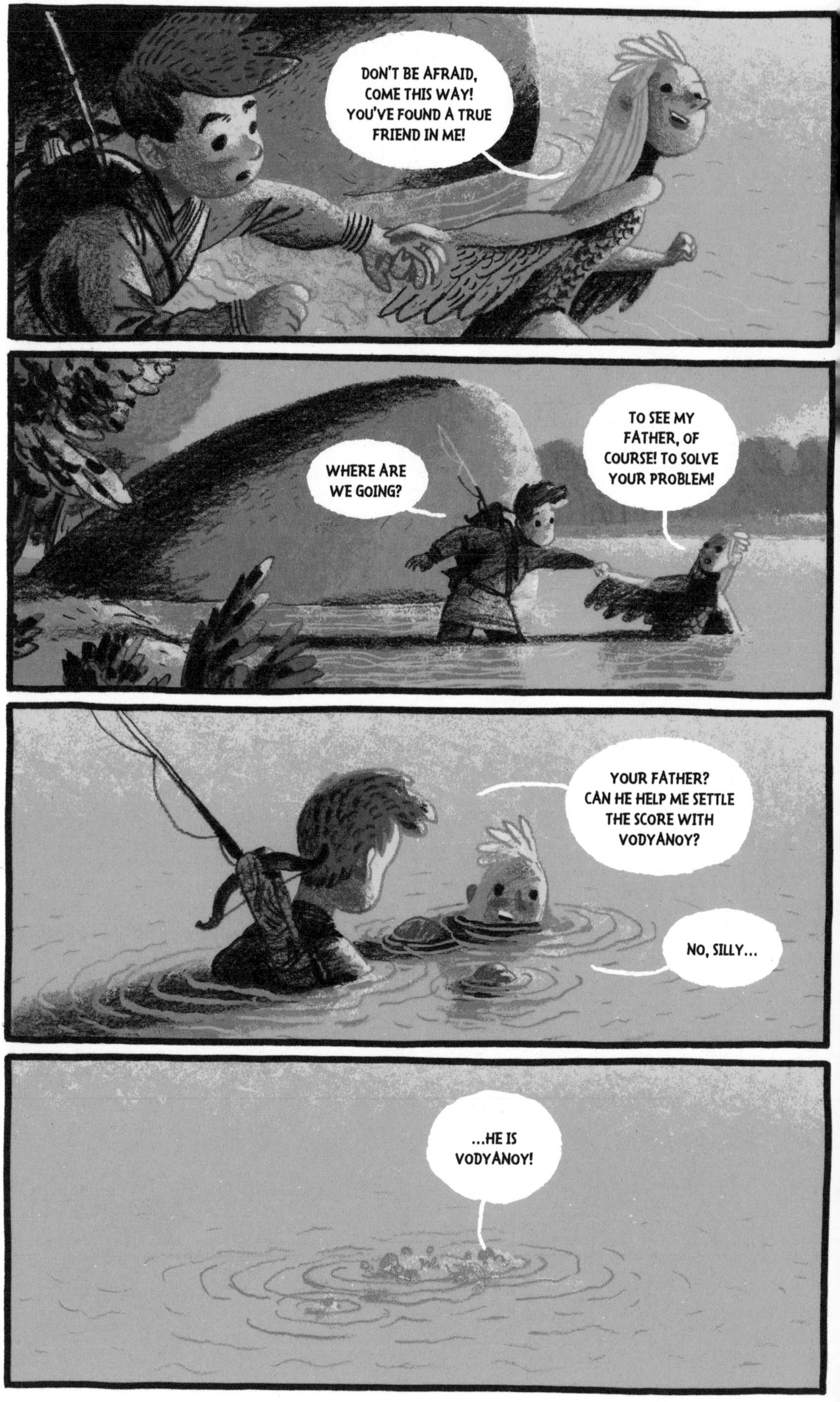
DON'T BE AFRAID, COME THIS WAY! YOU'VE FOUND A TRUE FRIEND IN ME!
WHERE ARE WE GOING?
TO SEE MY FATHER, OF COURSE! TO SOLVE YOUR PROBLEM!
YOUR FATHER? CAN HE HELP ME SETTLE THE SCORE WITH VODYANOY?
NO, SILLY...
...HE IS VODYANOY!

NEXT GAMAYUN TALE:

TYNA OF THE LAKE

WILL VODYANOY SPARE THE BOY FROM A LIFE OF SERVITUDE?
WHAT CHALLENGES AND ADVENTURES AWAIT TYNA AND
THE MERCHANT'S SON IN THE UNDERWATER KINGDOM?
AND WILL HE EVER BE REUNITED WITH HIS FAMILY?

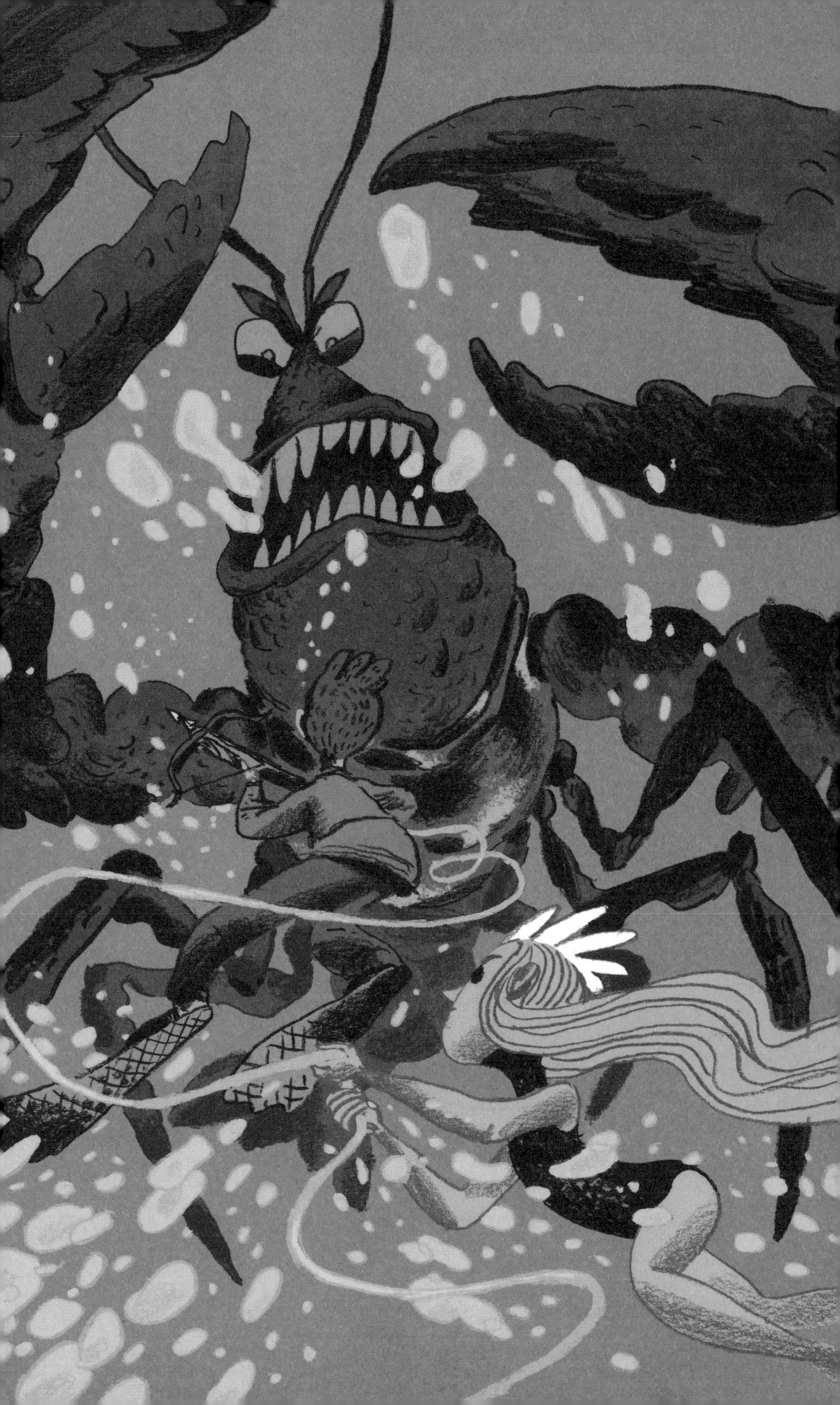

READ THE PREVIOUS
GAMAYUN TALE...

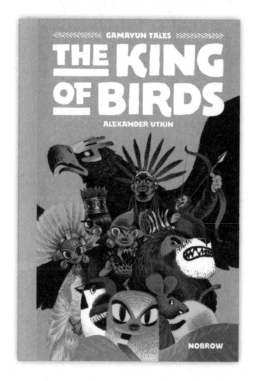

IBSN: 978-1-910620-38-0

THE WATER SPIRIT © NOBROW 2018.

THIS IS A FIRST EDITION PUBLISHED IN 2018 BY
NOBROW LTD. 27 WESTGATE STREET, LONDON E8 3RL.

TEXT AND ILLUSTRATIONS © ALEXANDER UTKIN 2018.

TRANSLATION BY LADA MOROZOVA.

ALEXANDER UTKIN HAS ASSERTED HIS RIGHT UNDER
THE COPYRIGHT, DESIGNS AND PATENTS ACT, 1988, TO BE IDENTIFIED
AS THE AUTHOR AND ILLUSTRATOR OF THIS WORK.

PUBLISHED IN THE US BY NOBROW (US) INC.

PRINTED IN LITHUANIA ON FSC® CERTIFIED PAPER.

ISBN: 978-1-910620-48-9

MIX
Paper from
responsible sources
FSC® C107574

ORDER FROM WWW.NOBROW.NET